'Surpr[ise],' [he said] quietly[.]

'I...what do you want? What are you doing here?'

'What do you think I'm doing here? We have some unfinished business, remember?'

He wasn't just angry, he was furious—a cold, icy fury, which made answering shivers trickle along her spine.

'Look, Mr Calder,' she began. 'I know you must be annoyed about what...'

'Annoyed? No, I'm not *annoyed*, Miss Williams, I'm furious!'

WE HOPE you're enjoying our new addition to our Contemporary Romance series—stories which take a light-hearted look at the Zodiac and show that love can be written in the stars!

Every month you can get to know a different combination of star-crossed lovers, with one story that follows the fortunes of a hero or a heroine when they embark on the romance of a lifetime with somebody born under another sign of the Zodiac. This month features a sizzling love-affair between **CAPRICORN** and **VIRGO**.

To find out more fascinating facts about this month's featured star sign, turn to the back pages of this book. . .

ABOUT THIS MONTH'S AUTHOR

Jennifer Taylor says: 'Capricorn and Virgo: I couldn't resist choosing these signs but what a shock when I started the research.

I had never realised that my need to be in control of a situation and tendency to over-work owed anything to being a Capricorn! Nor that my husband's desire for order and precision stems from him being a Virgo. It explains a lot. However, one thing I *do* know is that this combination of signs does work. . .romantically!'

DESTINED TO LOVE

BY

JENNIFER TAYLOR

MILLS & BOON LIMITED
ETON HOUSE 18–24 PARADISE ROAD
RICHMOND SURREY TW9 1SR

All the characters in this book have no existence outside the imagination of the Author, and have no relation whatsoever to anyone bearing the same name or names. They are not even distantly inspired by any individual known or unknown to the Author, and all the incidents are pure invention.

All Rights Reserved. The text of this publication or any part thereof may not be reproduced or transmitted in any form or by any means, electronic or mechanical, including photocopying, recording, storage in an information retrieval system, or otherwise, without the written permission of the publisher.

This book is sold subject to the condition that it shall not, by way of trade or otherwise, be lent, resold, hired out or otherwise circulated without the prior consent of the publisher in any form of binding or cover other than that in which it is published and without a similar condition including this condition being imposed on the subsequent purchaser.

First published in Great Britain 1992 by Mills & Boon Limited

© Jennifer Taylor 1992

*Australian copyright 1992
Philippine copyright 1992
This edition 1992*

ISBN 0 263 77840 1

STARSIGN ROMANCES is a trademark of Harlequin Enterprises B.V., Fribourg Branch. Mills and Boon is an authorised user.

*Set in 10 on 12 pt Linotron Times
01-9212-53363 Z*

*Typeset in Great Britain by Centracet, Cambridge
Made and printed in Great Britain*

CHAPTER ONE

IT WAS like grabbing a tiger by the tail!

The first tug had awoken him from a complacent slumber, the second had brought him to his feet. The question now was, what would the third achieve? There was only one way to find out.

Fran fixed a cool smile to her lips, her eyes running warily over the man seated opposite. He had agreed to the live radio interview readily enough, probably expecting it to run the course of a dozen or so others he'd done over the past couple of years. Only now had it occurred to him that it was moving along quite different channels.

Luke Calder was an important man. He was used to people listening to his opinions. That Fran had no intention of doing just that had only just struck him, and he didn't like it one little bit!

'So you feel that's enough, do you, Mr Calder? *Your* assurance that the whole area won't be destroyed by the development?' There was just a touch of sarcasm in her voice, which cut like a razor, and she knew she'd drawn blood when he stared coldly back at her, the smile fading from his face.

'Of course it's enough. I've given my word that, if I do decide to invest in this project, all care will be exercised to see that the area isn't spoiled in any way.'

'Yet surely just even planning this kind of a development entails a risk, an unacceptably high one, according to the residents. The land borders on the edge of the green belt, and the proposed development of houses, no matter how luxurious you intend them to be, will do nothing to enhance the area. It will mean added congestion on roads, which are barely adequate to cope with the present traffic, not to mention more people brought into what is now a pleasant rural area. And, of course, there's the golf course.'

She paused, feeling a shiver work its way down her spine as she met the black eyes that were regarding her so closely now. With his dark good looks, Luke Calder was a devastatingly attractive man, but right at that moment Fran was more concerned by the fact that he was watching her as though he would like to take her by her slender neck and shake her! But still, she hadn't got into this line of work to make friends. All she was concerned about was that people should know the truth and that justice should be served.

'What about the golf course, Miss Williams? I take it you aren't in favour of the idea?'

His voice was low, the deep tones carrying only the faintest hint of a Scottish accent that time and distance had helped him to shed. Fran had read all she could about Luke Calder before the interview and knew that he came from the poorest part of Glasgow and that he had got to where he was today by dint of sheer hard work and determination, but, looking at him now, she found it hard to imagine that he had come from anything but a moneyed background.

From the top of his sleek dark head to the tips of his expensive handmade leather shoes, he exuded an aura of wealth and power. It was only that faint burr in his voice which hinted at his background and made her realise that behind the elegant façade lay pure steel.

'I'm neither in favour of nor against the proposed golf-course, Mr Calder. I just wonder at the necessity of it in an area that already has two golf-courses to its credit. Obviously, I understand that this course is to be built mainly for the benefit of the people who'll buy the new houses, but it seems a pity that natural unspoilt countryside should be bulldozed to make way for what's really just a few rich people's pastime.'

'This area, Miss Williams, might encompass a few square miles of countryside, but it will also take in what is now a very unsightly rubbish tip. That whole site will be levelled and filled in, then re-landscaped as part of the golf-course. Are you really saying that you'd rather see a rubbish tip than fairways?'

He raised a mocking dark brow as he sat back in his seat and crossed one long leg over the other, and Fran bit back a sudden urge to snap an answer at him. She would get nowhere by being goaded into letting this interview degenerate into a clash of personalities, although the temptation was growing increasingly great.

'Of course I'm not, Mr Calder. I think you're trying to over-simplify the matter. However, one thing that you can't over-simplify is the fact that the old theological college will have to be knocked down before you can go ahead. Can you really justify the destruction of such a fine old building?'

'I wonder how long it's been since you visited that fine old building, Miss Williams! The college has fallen into a state of such disrepair since it was closed down that I doubt if anyone could truthfully class it as that.'

He smiled infuriatingly at her, lifting a hand to run it over his dark hair, seemingly as relaxed as though they were just sharing a pleasant little chat rather than this frosty interview. 'However, in deference to public opinion, the developers have decided to see if it would be at all possible to have the building renovated and brought back to its former glory. You obviously weren't aware of that fact, I see.'

'I. . . No.' She ground her teeth, glaring down at the neat stack of notes before her on the desk. Debbie in Research would have a lot of explaining to do to get around this! She drew in a deep breath, shooting a glance at the large clock opposite her, wishing the interview was over. She was usually so confident when dealing with even the most difficult of guests on the *Day-to-Day* programme, but there was just something about Luke Calder that seemed to throw her off balance. Maybe she would be better advised to try a different approach. 'That's welcome news, of course, but I doubt that it will remove all the very real concerns that abound in the community. This is a smallish town, Mr Calder. I'm sure you can appreciate that people are wary of big-city developers coming in and turning everywhere upside-down because they know nothing about the area.'

'Of course I can. That's one of the reasons why I decided to get involved in the project in the first place when it was first broached to me. This isn't just another investment opportunity for me, you see, Miss Williams. I also have a personal interest in seeing that the development goes ahead in a way that will only enhance the town.'

'Personal? I'm sorry, but I don't quite follow you

there. How can this development be of any personal interest to you?'

'I see this is another aspect of it you're unaware of, Miss Williams. I'm surprised. I was led to believe that your programme was noted for its in-depth research of the facts. But no matter—this has no real bearing on the development, but may be of some interest to those in the community who see this as just another get-rich-quick venture by the men from the city. I used to live in this town when I was a very small child, Miss Williams. My mother came from around here, and we lived in the area until I was about eight years old. It's always held a special meaning for me, and when the development is completed I have every intention of moving back into the area and making my home here. So, as you can imagine, I would be loath to do anything to finance a venture that would be detrimental to the town or the community.'

Fran was furious. She could feel the anger surging inside her and she fought it down, not wanting him to know what a fool she felt for not having been made aware of that fact. 'I see. Well, maybe that will be faintly reassuring for one or two people, but I'm sure you'll understand if I reserve judgement for now.' She flicked him a perfunctory smile, seeing the mockery lingering in his dark eyes in a way that made her itch to reach out and slap him. The thought shocked her rigid. She had always prided herself on her calm, her coolness under pressure, yet twenty minutes of Luke Calder's company and she was ready to act like a harpy!

'Twenty seconds, Fran.'

The voice of the controller came clearly through the

headphones, and she waved a hand in acknowledgement, then started winding the programme up. 'Well, that's just about it, I think, Mr Calder. We're about to run out of time. I would like to thank you for coming into the studio today, and I'm sure we'll receive a lot of letters from our listeners about what's been said. You could find that this is just the beginning and that your plans aren't quite as cut and dried as they appear.'

'Thank you, Miss Williams. I'll be interested to hear any views from the community. We might both be surprised that they aren't quite all as one-sided as you think they are.'

Fran glared at him, cursing the fact that he had managed to get the last word on *her* programme! She waited until the first few bars of the signature tune started to play, then unclipped her headphones and set them down on the desk with a sharp clatter before starting to gather up the stack of notes.

'Allow me.' He reached past her to pick up the papers, a faint smile curling his chiselled lips as he scanned the typewritten sheets.

'If you don't mind, those are private.' Fran held her hand out, annoyance in every line of her face as she glared coldly at him, but he seemed unperturbed.

'I fail to see how they can be private when they're about me.' He read to the bottom of the sheet, then turned the page, laughing softly as he read on.

'And what exactly is so amusing? Have we got a few more facts wrong?'

'No, I can honestly say that the facts are correct: I am thirty-two, I did live for many years in Scotland, and yes, I do head one of the largest investment corporations in the country.' He held the notes out to her, but didn't relinquish them when she reached out her hand. Just for a moment their eyes met, and Fran experienced the most incredible feeling of dizziness until determinedly she brought herself back under control.

'Well, I'm glad to know that we've achieved that much at least,' she snapped.

'Oh, you have. But what I can't understand is why you needed to know what star sign I am, or the characteristics that go with it. Is it standard policy to include facts like that in your research?'

The amusement in his voice stung, and she snatched the papers from him and stuffed them deep into the pocket of her briefcase. Damn Debbie for doing that, for including such ridiculous information when she could barely manage to glean the facts!

'Unfortunately my research assistant is prone to these flights of fancy. However, let me assure you that your star sign had little bearing on how I conducted the interview.' She snapped the locks on the case, lifting it from the table, wanting only to get away from Luke Calder as fast as she could.

'You think not?' He smiled almost gently, but there was nothing gentle about the glitter in his dark eyes as they ran over her from the smooth shining coil of her silver-blonde hair to the long slender legs encased in elegant sheer navy stockings. 'My mother was a great believer in horoscopes all her life. She liked nothing better than to try to match a stranger's characteristics and behaviour with a particular sign, then try to find out if she was right.'

'How interesting. Now, if you'll excuse me, Mr Calder, I'm very busy.'

Fran tried to step past him, but he just stood where he was, making no attempt to get out of her way while he continued to study her in a way that made her suddenly self-conscious. Her hand reached up to smooth her already immaculate hair before she let it drop abruptly when she saw the amusement on his face. She had dressed with extra care that morning and knew that she looked her best in the slim-fitting navy suit with a spotless white blouse, but it was disconcerting to be subjected to such a scrutiny.

'Virgo.'

'I beg your pardon?' She took a step backwards, staring at him as though he had suddenly gone mad.

'Your star sign. . . Virgo. Am I right?'

'I. . . That's none of your business! Now I really must go. Thank you for coming on the show today, Mr Calder.' She held her hand out, feeling a shiver ripple up her spine when his long fingers closed around hers.

'Thank you, Miss Williams. It was a pleasure crossing wits with you.' He turned to go, then stopped, looking back at where she was standing staring down at her hand. 'I don't know whether you've really read all those extensive notes your researcher made for you, but do take a look at the last couple of lines. They could prove. . .interesting.'

He left the studio, the padded door swinging to with a soft thud. Fran drew in a slow deep breath, feeling the tension flowing from her limbs. Never had she felt so on edge before or during an interview—or after, for that matter! There was just something about Luke Calder that seemed to affect her, although for the life of her she couldn't understand what it was. What had he meant about the last couple of lines of her notes?

She had barely skimmed over the last few paragraphs of information, used to Debbie's ridiculous ideas about a person's birth sign giving a clue to his character, but now the temptation to find out proved too great.

Setting the briefcase back down, she dug the notes out of the pocket and turned to the last page, smiling rather nastily. So he was Capricorn, was he? The sign of the goat. How apt, especially when one considered the traits allotted to that particular sign. Ambitious, calculating, ruthless...well, they summed up Luke Calder to a T! Fran read on, deriving some measure of comfort from the less than flattering assessment, although in truth she knew that she was deliberately glossing over the more attractive aspects of the sign. Maybe there *was* something in this astrology after all, if...

Her eyes widened as she came to the last paragraph, and she stared at it before abruptly crumpling the paper and stuffing it back into her case. It had thrown her when Luke Calder had made that seemingly wild guess about her, but now she could understand it. She would have to have a stern talk with Debbie about including extraneous information instead of plain hard fact.

Embarrassment curled hotly through her as she remembered what she'd read and she snatched up the case and marched towards the door, but it wasn't that easy to push it from her mind, not when she remembered Luke Calder's mockery.

The Capricorn will often find him or herself attracted to a partner born under the sign of Virgo, as both signs are complementary to each other. Watch out, Fran... Virgo is your sign!

Well, that just proved what a lot of mumbo-jumbo it all was, because the last thing that had happened had been that Luke infuriating Calder had exhibited any signs of being attracted to her...and vice versa!

'You were pushing it a bit today, Fran. Do you think it was wise to get Calder's back up like that?'

Fran glanced up from the pile of newscuttings on her desk. 'Probably not, Fred. Did it sound as bad as it felt?'

Fred shrugged, his lined face creasing into a wry smile. 'It wasn't one of the best interviews you've ever done. What happened? Didn't you hit it off?'

'You could say that.' She sighed, putting down her pencil. 'No, that's just an excuse. I allowed my personal dislike of the man to surface when I should have remained detached. Mind you, the fact that Debbie had missed all those vital details didn't help. I felt such a fool when he picked me up like that. I tell you, Fred, letting Debbie do my research just isn't working. I'm seriously thinking about going back to doing it myself!'

'You haven't got the time. Fronting the programme is hard enough without having to do all the leg work as well. She'll settle down all right. Just give her time.'

'All right, but there's no way I'm entrusting this story about Harry Martin to her. There's too much at stake.' Fran glanced back at the heap of cuttings, frowning as she sorted through the pile. 'I know there's a link there somewhere between Martin and someone at the town hall. There's no other way to explain the fact that he's been allowed to buy that land so cheaply. It's just proving it that's going to be difficult. Most of the councillors seem to be hand in glove with each other; you can't make any one of them speak to you, let alone give an interview.'

'I know. It's some sort of fraud all right. That's the only explanation for it, but you try proving it. . . Maybe you should let it drop, love. It might be more trouble than it's worth.'

'Let it drop? No way! If we did that then face it, Fred, we'd end up like a dozen other so-called topical news programmes. Our audience deserves better than that from us.'

She glared at the older man, her grey eyes gleaming with determination, and saw him smile.

'I had a feeling that you might say that, but I just thought I'd better check it out. It won't be easy, Fran. Martin's a slippery customer, a very *nasty* slippery customer. You're going to have to be careful how you handle this.'

'I shall.' She scooped the cuttings into a pile and tucked them back into their folder before standing up. 'Look, I think I'll take this lot home with me and go through them later tonight. I feel a bit jaded right now, but I'll feel better after a meal and a hot bath.'

'Well, don't work too late. You know the old saying about all work and no play?'

'Are you accusing me of being dull? Shame on you, Fred, and I thought you were my friend! No, I just need to go through these all by myself without any interruptions and see if anything clicks into place. After all, I don't want to let the rest of the team down.'

'The rest of the team know what a good job you're doing, Fran. You don't have to keep proving yourself.'

'Maybe not, but I know there was a lot of opposition from the guys when a woman was put in the hot seat.'

'They might have given you a rough ride at first, but you survived—more than survived! You're a lot tougher than you look.' Fred's eyes swept over her delicate features and slender figure with such a wry look that she had to laugh. It hadn't been easy to break into the tough world of radio news reporting, not with her fragile appearance, which had always been such a handicap. However, Fran now felt that she was being accepted as part of the team. She just didn't want to give anyone the chance to put her down. The job was important to her; it had been the goal she had set herself after her father died so tragically ten years ago when she was seventeen. Then she had sworn to find some way to fight injustice and make sure that no one else suffered the way he had done. Working on the *Day-to-Day* show was her chance to do just that.

'I'm glad you've all finally realised it. I got a bit tired of being treated like Dresden china.' She picked up the file and her briefcase. 'Right, I shall see you tomorrow.'

'Fine. Oh, just one thing before you go, Fran. Are you planning a follow-up to today's programme to give Calder a chance to respond to any letters that come in? You know the sort of thing.'

'No!' She eased the sharpness from her voice, aware that Fred was looking at her in surprise. 'I don't think that will be necessary. We'll let it lie for now, and if we do get any kind of a big response then maybe we can think about scheduling another programme, but I can't honestly see that happening.'

'I'd have thought you'd jump at the chance to have a second shot at the man.'

A shudder ran through her at the thought of meeting Luke Calder again and she turned away, making a great performance of picking up her handbag. 'I don't see that Mr Calder and I have anything more to discuss.'

She left the office, ignoring the speculative look Fred gave her. Wild horses wouldn't make her ask what had caused it, not when she had the uncomfortable feeling that she wouldn't enjoy hearing the answer! As far as she was concerned, today was the first and last time that she and Luke Calder would ever meet.

It was already late afternoon. Fran hurried across the street, weaving her way between the busy traffic towards the underground car park favoured by the staff at the radio station. There was talk of the whole station's being moved into purpose-built accommodation some time in the future, but so far nothing definite had been arranged, so they were forced to put up with the cramped conditions and lack of amenities, like parking.

Now, as she hurried into the dimly lit tunnel to the ground-floor area where they all parked their cars, she quickened her pace, uneasy as always about the poor lighting and the feeling of being cut off if she should need help. There had been several nasty incidents recently in the town when lone women had been subjected to attacks of one kind or another, so she couldn't help but look over her shoulder as she made her way along the rows of parked cars to where her small Fiesta was parked next to a sleek-looking Jaguar.

Pausing for a moment to admire the trim lines of the expensive vehicle, she dug in her bag for her keys, then muttered in annoyance as they slid from her fingers. Hitching up the skirt of her suit, Fran knelt down to retrieve them, then felt a shaft of fear run through her when she heard footsteps coming up behind her.

She scrambled to her feet, feeling her heart bump painfully as she caught sight of the two men standing by the car. Although both were impeccably dressed in dark suits, there was just something about them that reminded Fran of the old wolf in sheep's clothing story. Frankly, neither looked like the kind of man that a woman would want to meet in a dark street. . .or even darker car park.

'Miss Williams?'

Startled, her eyes shot to the man who had spoken. 'Yes.'

'We have a message for you, Miss Williams.'

'A message. . .what sort of a message? What are you talking about?' There was a slight shrillness to her voice and she bit her lip to contain the rising feeling of panic. Hurriedly she glanced round, assessing her chances of getting away if she made a run for it, then started nervously when the second man took a deliberate step sideways to effectively block her path. He grinned at her, his fleshy lips curled into a knowing line, and Fran felt the first stirrings of anger damp down on the fear.

How dared he grin at her like that? In fact, how dared they waylay her like this? 'Now look here, if you have a message then tell me what it is. I have no intention of standing here playing games!'

'We're not playing games, Miss Williams. Rest assured that we're deadly serious.'

There was a nasty emphasis on the last words, but Fran strove hard to ignore it and keep the alarm from her voice. 'Then what are you playing at? What is this message, and, more to the point, who is it from?' She took a quick step forward and saw the flicker of surprise on the man's face. Obviously he had thought that the mere sight of them would frighten her into standing quietly and listening, but he was wrong. She was scared all right, but not so scared that she was going to meekly stand there!

'I asked you a question. Shall I repeat it? Who is this message from?'

He seemed to hesitate for a moment. 'Let's just call him a friend, shall we?'

'I see, and does this "friend" have a name? Or can't you manage to remember it?'

There was an edge of sarcasm in her voice, which she immediately regretted when she saw the anger flicker across his face.

'No, he doesn't have a name as far as you're concerned. So let's cut out all the smart answers, shall we, lady, if you know what's good for you?'

There was no mistaking the menace in his demeanour as he advanced towards her, and Fran took several hasty steps backwards before coming to an abrupt halt against the wall.

'Now you look here. . .'

'No, *you* look here. In fact, why don't you just keep quiet before I lose my patience? The message from my friend is this: that you should keep that pretty little nose out of things that don't concern you if you don't want to find yourself in a whole load of trouble. Understand?' He moved closer, and Fran shuddered as he ran a finger softly down the straight little bridge of her nose. 'It would be a shame to see such pretty packaging spoilt, wouldn't it, sweetheart? So why not be a sensible girl and——?'

'Fran! Darling, I've been looking everywhere for you!'

A hand reached past the man and caught her arm, pulling her away from the wall, away from the sickening touch of those fingers on her skin. Fran caught her breath, completely stunned by this turn of events. For one speechless moment she stared up into a pair of devil-dark eyes, then abruptly came to her senses and tried to break away.

'What do you think you——?'

'Now, now, my love, don't be cross. I know I'm late, but I really couldn't help it. Forgive me. . .please?'

The fingers tightened round her arm, biting deep into her flesh as she continued to struggle, and Fran knew as clearly as she knew her own name that he had no intention of letting her go. Anger roared inside her and she opened her mouth to tell him in no uncertain terms where to go, only she didn't have a chance to utter even one heated word, as he bent and covered her parted lips with his, kissing her with a thoroughness that left her shaken.

She couldn't seem to move, to speak, to do anything apart from stand there in Luke Calder's arms. . .and let him kiss her!

CHAPTER TWO

To FRAN'S undying shame, it was Luke Calder who broke off the kiss. Raising his head, he looked past her to where the two men were standing, seemingly as bemused by his sudden intervention as she was herself.

'Sorry. I didn't mean to butt in, but we're already late, thanks to me getting lost. I'm sure you'll understand if I whisk Fran away with me now.'

His voice was low, easy, the faint accent she'd barely noticed before more pronounced now, unless it was just that her senses had been heightened by that devastatingly thorough kiss. He appeared relaxed, yet there was nothing relaxed about the taut feel of the muscles where her hands were resting against his chest, nothing relaxed about the biting grip of the fingers spanning her waist. The realisation made her hesitate when indignation demanded that she should move away. She had no idea what he was up to, but instinct told her that he was trying to help her, and in this case it seemed wiser to follow her instincts.

Warily Fran glanced over her shoulder at the two men. Would they accept what he had said and let them go rather than cause a scene? The thought of having to continue that conversation was so alarming that unconsciously she moved closer to Luke Calder, finding comfort in the solid feel of his hard-muscled body.

He glanced down at her, his dark eyes crinkling at the corners as he smiled in a way that made her heart turn a tiny somersault. Bending, he feathered a kiss along her cheek, his cool lips pausing at the delicate curve of her ear. 'Stop looking like a frightened little rabbit. It'll be all right now that I'm here.'

His voice was low, for her alone, but it did the trick. Fran stiffened, glaring up at him, hating him for his cool self-assurance, but he ignored the look as his hands tightened painfully around her waist in a silent warning not to do anything silly, before he spoke again, louder this time for the benefit of their audience. 'Ready, then, darling? I think it's time we were on our way.'

He urged her forward, turning her towards the passenger door of the sleek Jaguar before handing her inside and closing the door. Fran settled herself in the soft leather seat, not daring to glance at the two men in case she precipitated some sort of an adverse reaction. It seemed unbelievable that they would stand aside and let them leave like this.

Holding her breath, she waited while Luke Calder walked round and climbed behind the wheel, starting the engine before glancing sideways at her with a mocking little smile. 'Oh, ye of little faith. Didn't I tell you it would be all right?'

Fran sucked in a deep breath, fighting the double urge to weep with relief and slap the smile off his mocking face. Instead she contented herself with glaring coldly at him as she fastened the seatbelt. 'We're not in the clear yet. What happens if those two goons have a sudden change of heart and decide not to let us go? I doubt if you can kiss your way out of that!'

He laughed. 'I doubt if I'd want to. I'm particular about whom I kiss, and neither of that pair has a single one of your assets. Now give your friends a nice big smile and a wave, and let's get out of here before they have a chance to think it all through.'

He reversed out of the parking space, and Fran fixed a determined smile to her face—then gasped in dismay when the man who had done all the talking stepped into their path. He tapped on the window, and she had to force herself not to cringe as Luke Calder pressed a button on the dashboard and it slid down.

'Don't forget what I told you, Miss Williams. My friend is very anxious about your welfare. He wouldn't like to see any harm come to you.'

Fran swallowed hard, feeling the bitter taste of fear burning her throat as she stared into the man's cold, flat eyes, wishing she could find her voice to tell him what he could do with his threats.

'You don't need to worry about Miss Williams's welfare, and neither does your "friend". I shall see that no harm comes to her. Perhaps you can pass that message on for me!'

Fran turned in her seat, her eyes racing to Luke Calder's face, and a shiver worked its way down her spine. She'd thought before that he seemed used to power, and looking at him now only served to strengthen that feeling. Luke Calder would be a bad man to cross, and suddenly she was glad that this time he was on her side and not the opposition's.

Abruptly the window slid upwards and the car shot forward, forcing the man outside to take a hasty step back. Fran had just enough time to catch a glimpse of the anger on his face, then they were past, heading for the exit ramp at breakneck speed. Bright evening sunlight glared through the windscreen, dazzling her after the gloom, and she raised a hand to shade her eyes just as Luke Calder turned the car into the road, cutting in front of a lorry so close that her stomach lurched.

'Do you have to drive so fast?' she snapped.

'Yes. I don't fancy playing tag along the road with those guys, even if you do, so stop complaining.'

'Oh.' She twisted round in the seat but could see no sign of a pursuing car. 'Do you really think they'll follow us?'

He shrugged, feeding the steering-wheel expertly through his hands as they roared round a corner. 'Who knows? Let's just say that I deem it wiser to get a head start on them.'

'But what shall we do if they do follow us?'

'I'd have thought you'd be a better judge of that than me.'

'What on earth do you mean?' Startled, Fran shot him a quick look.

'Simply that if you've got yourself into some sort of a mess then that's your business. But I would have imagined that an intelligent woman like you would know how to get herself out of it again.'

'How to. . . Now look here! I don't know what you're implying, but, for your information, I have no idea what those goons wanted. I've done nothing to put myself in a position where I have. . .hit men coming after me!'

Angry indignation laced her voice, but he appeared unmoved. 'Maybe you're pure and white as the driven snow, but you have to face the fact that there must be some reason why those men waylaid you. Listen, I know their sort, and take my word for it that they're professionals. They don't go around trying to frighten people just for pleasure. Someone paid them good money, a lot of money, to do that—this so-called "friend" they mentioned—so if I were you I'd be trying to work out who he is rather than getting on my soapbox. You've got yourself in somebody's bad books, my girl, so think hard who it is.'

It made sense, although she hated to admit it. But who would have gone to such lengths to scare her, and why? She sat back in the seat as she racked her brain before coming to just one conclusion: Harry Martin. Who else had the money and the connections to hire men like that? Who else stood to gain so much if she could be frightened into staying quiet? He had a reputation in the town for dirty dealing, but surely this sort of thing was carrying things too far, even for him? He couldn't really think that she would stop her investigations just because of a few threats?

'Any ideas yet?' asked Luke. 'The best way to rout the enemy is to confront him, but you can't do that until you know his name.' There was the harsh edge of authority in his deep voice now as he demanded an answer, but Fran ignored it. None of this was his business, despite the fact that he had helped her out of a rather. . .tricky situation.

'I'm not sure,' she shrugged.

'But you do have some idea who it could be?'

'Perhaps.'

'Something to do with your work, I imagine. You do seem to have a propensity for rubbing people up the wrong way.'

'All I do is report the facts, Mr Calder. What people make of them is their business, and if they have something to hide then you can't expect me to weep for them.'

'Facts...like all those facts you had on those sheets this morning?' There was a cold, hard mockery in his face as he glanced over at her, and she stiffened.

'I mean facts that relate to the story I'm working on at the time. I can hardly be held accountable for the vagaries of a junior research assistant!'

'Maybe not, but if I were you, Miss Williams, I'd make sure that I confined myself to facts in future, and the most pressing one of all is the *fact* that someone in this town is annoyed with you!'

'So what do you suggest? That I should back off from a story that I *know* needs to be brought out into the open? I didn't go into this line of work to take the easy option every time things get rough. If the public needs to be made aware of what's going on then I shall be the one to do it, and no one...no one will scare me off from reporting the truth!'

'How very noble, but don't you think you're taking too much on, and for what? A few minutes of air time on a small radio station? You're hardly going to change the world by what you do, so why risk another confrontation like that last one? There might not be anyone around willing to come to your aid next time.'

His tone stung, the cool calculation in the advice annoying her intensely. A typical Capricorn characteristic, if Debbie's notes had been accurate in any way at all!

'Come to my aid? You call those sneaky, underhand tactics coming to my aid? Hah!'

Fran regretted her hasty words the very moment she saw the way his mouth thinned into a cold anger. He pulled the car over to the kerb and let the engine idle while he turned to face her. Sunlight streamed through the windscreen, settling burnished rays over his black hair, turning his olive complexion to gold so that for a moment his face took on the appearance of a mask. Only his eyes seemed alive, burning with a dark fire as he stared at her. Deep down she knew that she should apologise for what she had said, but she'd had enough today to last her a lifetime!

She stared back at him, refusing to give an inch, then jumped when he leant forward to run a finger softly down the smooth curve of her cheek.

'Sneaky, underhand tactics, were they?' Luke said softly, his voice so deep that it seemed to run along her nerves and play a tune like a violin. 'Maybe they were sneaky, maybe they were underhand, but at the time I didn't notice you objecting to them.'

It took a second for the words to sink home, but when they did she jerked her head back and swatted his hand away. 'Yes, they were sneaky and underhand. If you were so set on helping me then why didn't you just come straight over and. . .'

'And what? Challenge them to a good old-fashioned fist fight? I hate to disillusion you, but I'd have been hard pressed to come out on top with those odds!'

'And that would go against the grain, wouldn't it. . . to do anything without working out the odds first?' Fran stared coldly at him. 'However, let's just get something straight here and now, shall we? I never asked you to step in back there. What you did you did of your own free choice. Frankly, I had the situation well under control before you even appeared on the scene!'

How she didn't choke on the blatant lie, she had no idea, but she didn't. She smiled calmly back at him, her teeth snapping together when he just laughed in open disbelief. 'Under control! That's rich, really rich! That pair had you cornered, and heaven alone knew what they intended to do next if I hadn't risked both life and limb by stepping in to help you. So don't give me that line, because I'm not buying it!'

'I have no intention of giving you anything apart from one little word. . .goodbye! Oh, and maybe just a tiny piece of advice: next time you, quote, "risk life and limb" I suggest you check first that the person does need rescuing. That way you could save yourself a whole load of trouble, not to mention planning!'

She smiled sweetly, opening the car door to get out, then stopped abruptly when his fingers closed around her arm.

'Where do you think you're off to?' he demanded, his tone so hard that involuntarily she shivered.

'That's none of your business. Now take your hand off my arm.' Fran jerked her arm away but it did little to loosen the crushing grip of his powerful fingers. Suddenly unease rose inside her and she faltered as a sudden thought struck her. She had taken his intervention at face value, but perhaps the whole incident had been planned, deliberately, as a way to inveigle himself into her good books. She had assumed that Harry Martin was behind it all, but who was to say if Luke Calder hadn't coldly and calculatedly planned the whole thing?

Anger gave her an added surge of strength, and she twisted her arm sharply downwards and broke his grip. She jumped out of the car and hurried along the road, ignoring the colourful epithet that followed her. Behind her she could hear the sudden roar of the car engine as he pulled away from the kerb, then the steady throb as he slowed it alongside her.

'For heaven's sake, stop being so stupid. Get back in here at once!'

Like hell she would! Gritting her teeth against the acid flow of retorts, Fran hurried on, quickening her pace almost to a run in an attempt to get away, but he just drove along beside her.

'What do you think this will achieve? All you're doing is causing us both a whole lot of inconvenience by this irrational behaviour.'

'Then go away, and that way I won't cause you any more inconvenience at all!' She glared at him, then scanned the road for anyone who might offer help if he turned nasty and tried to force her back inside the car, but, apart from an elderly woman walking an equally elderly terrier along the opposite pavement, the road was deserted. Still, there was safety in numbers, even sparse ones, so she skipped smartly across the street, shortening her stride to keep pace with the woman's slower one.

With a noisy roar the car shot across the road and crawled along next to her, travelling against the oncoming flow of traffic. 'What the hell's got into you? What if those men are following us? You're giving them the perfect opportunity to cut in again.'

'And why would you expect them to be following? Because you're the one who put them up to it? The only person I can see following me is you. Now go away!'

'I put them. . .? Now hold on there! What kind of

stupid ideas have got into your head now? Just quit acting like the silly, irresponsible female you undoubtedly are and get in this car before I get out and make you!'

'How dare you threaten me? I have no intention whatsoever of getting in that car with you, so get that into your head once and for all. Now leave me alone!'

Fran's voice rose to a shrill scream, and the elderly woman who had been watching them curiously stopped. Looping the dog's lead over a handy gatepost, she came back.

'Is this man pestering you, dear?'

Fran nodded, too incensed by what Luke had said to frame a proper answer. How dared he call her a silly, irresponsible. . .? Her jaw dropped as the woman walked past her and stopped by the car.

'Men like you need locking up, do you hear? Locking up and the key throwing away! Bothering decent young women with your nasty perverted suggestions! You should be ashamed!'

'Look, I think you have this all wrong. I wasn't——'

'I have nothing wrong, young man. I heard you trying to persuade and then threaten this young lady to get her into your car, and it's not the first time I've witnessed such a thing. If I had my way then kerb-crawlers like you would be locked away! Now you have two minutes to be on your way before you have the police to answer to!'

Digging into the pocket of her jacket, she produced a long silver whistle and placed it firmly between her lips, and Fran had to swallow an almost hysterical gurgle of laughter as she saw the expression of near-disbelief on Luke Calder's face. Then as the first shrill blast pierced the air he slammed the car into gear and glared at her.

'You haven't heard the end of this,' he ground out, his eyes black as pitch as they locked on her face. 'Don't think I'll let you get away with it!'

The car drove off with a scream of tyres, and Fran shivered in sudden reaction as she watched him go.

'Well, that soon sorted him out, didn't it, dear? If I were you, though, I'd get straight on home just in case he comes back. I don't think I'd like to try crossing swords with him again. He doesn't look like the sort of man one can get the better of very often.'

Fran murmured her thanks as the woman collected the dog and went on her way, but it was a few minutes before she followed her. That brief confrontation with Luke Calder had unsettled her far more than the incident in the garage, if she was honest. She closed her eyes, shuddering as she remembered the expression on his face just before he had driven away, and, unbidden, the words that Debbie had typed came flooding back.

Luke Calder was a coolly calculating, ruthless man who would stop at nothing to get where or what he wanted. Whether it was pure coincidence or something deeper in his make-up, Fran had no idea. All she did know was that she hadn't seen the last of him by a long chalk!

Lights were spilling across the pavement when she finally arrived home. She walked up the path and leant wearily against the wall while she dug in her bag for her key, then groaned when she remembered that it was still lying on the floor of the car park where she had dropped it. She hurried next door to get the spare one she always left with her neighbour, then let herself inside and sank down wearily on the bottom of the stairs.

What on earth had prompted her to act like that tonight and get Luke Calder's back well and truly up? Now that she had had time to think everything through on the long walk home, she had soon realised how ridiculous her accusations must have sounded. Common sense should have told her that he hadn't had the time, even if he'd had the inclination, to arrange that visit from those two men. Mind you, common sense hadn't stood much of a chance from the very moment that he had appeared and kissed her. What was it about that infuriating man that made her act so out of character?

The telephone rang, mercifully cutting short any more disturbing thoughts, and she picked up the receiver. 'Hello?'

'Fran? Thank heavens you're back at last!'

'Fred? What's wrong? Why did you want me?'

'Because I've been worried sick ever since I saw your car.'

'My car? What's wrong with it?'

'You mean you don't know? I hate to be the bearer of bad tidings, so to speak, but it's been virtually wrecked—tyres slashed, windows smashed...the works.'

'Oh, no!' Fran sank weakly back against the stairs, trying to digest the information.

'I'm afraid so. I was worried sick when I saw it, and I've been ringing your number on and off for the past hour. Have you any idea what's been going on?'

'I think I do. There were a couple of men waiting for me in the car park tonight, said they had a message for me from a "friend" that ran along the lines of warning me to keep my nose out of things that didn't concern me.'

'You're joking!'

'I wish I were. It seems they must have had more than just a message. They must have wrecked the car to make sure that I understood they meant business.'

'I can scarcely believe this! Have you any idea who sent them? Did they give this "friend's" name?'

'No, but I've been giving it a lot of thought, and it seems to me that the person who fits the bill is. . .'

'Harry Martin,' Fred put in.

'So you think so too?'

'Who else? It has all his hallmarks, Fran. I know that nothing has ever been proved against the man, but you've heard the rumours about how he tries to pressurise people.'

'That's why I reached the same conclusion. Of course, I did wonder for a while if Lu. . .' She tailed off, cursing herself for the slip.

'What's that? Is there someone else you suspect?' Fred's voice was sharp with suspicion, and Fran knew that he would give her no peace unless she explained.

'Luke Calder,' she said quietly.

'Calder? Why on earth should you link him to this?'

'Because he arrived out of the blue and did his Sir Galahad act by getting me away from the men. It suddenly seemed too. . .well, too coincidental.'

'No, I think you're wrong about Calder. I know he has a reputation for toughness that could match Martin's any day, but the difference is that everything he does is legal and above board. There has never been any hint that he's been involved in underhand dealings.'

'I suppose you're right.'

'I know I am. But what took you so long getting home? Didn't Calder bring you?'

'He did, but we had a slight disagreement on the way. I virtually accused him of being the one responsible for sending the men to meet me.'

'You never did?' Fred laughed. 'Well, Fran, you certainly know how to choose your enemies—first Martin and now Luke Calder! It's hard to say which one will take the most careful handling, especially in view of the fact that Calder is reported to be considering backing the building of the new radio station. If he does then it will almost certainly mean that he'll be offered a directorship. So you could find that in a few months' time he's your boss.'

Could it get any worse? She doubted it. 'Thanks, Fred. That really does put my mind at ease!'

'It's always better to face the facts, Fran, you know that. Still, don't worry too much about it. I doubt if Calder will take it any further once he's had time to think it over and realise how upset you were. I'll see you tomorrow, then.'

He rang off, and Fran slowly replaced the receiver, wishing she felt as confident as Fred sounded about Luke Calder's eventual understanding. The trouble was that Fred had no real idea of what had gone on tonight, but she had!

Resting her head wearily against the hard banister rail, she fought down the momentary surge of panic. Let Luke Calder do what he liked. It made no difference to her aims in life. She hadn't got this far nor worked this hard just to give up at the thought of some sort of opposition. It wasn't only goats that would struggle up and over any obstacles in their paths!

CHAPTER THREE

'AND don't forget, Debbie, I want facts. . .plain, hard facts, and no more of this fanciful rubbish from now on!'

'Yes, Fr. . . Miss Williams.'

Debbie's pert little features settled into a mutinous line as she bent over her typewriter, and Fran sighed as she turned on her heel and left the room.

Maybe she could have handled that a little more tactfully instead of sounding as though she was throwing her weight around. The trouble was, she didn't feel *tactful*. She felt awful, tired, on edge, a dull throbbing ache pounding in her temples. All night long she had lain awake, worrying about what had happened and wishing with the benefit of hindsight that she had handled it better, but nothing could change what had gone on. She had well and truly burned her boats as far as Luke Calder was concerned, so pity help her if the rumours about his investing in the radio station were right. He could make life very difficult for her if he became one of the directors.

Lips compressed into a thin line of tension, she strode along the corridor and into her office, wrinkling her nose at the musty smell of stale air. She crossed the room and flung the window open, then sneezed as the sudden breeze sent dust motes dancing in the air.

'Bless you!'

She swung round so abruptly that she knocked a pot

of pencils off the desk with her hand. They fell to the floor and rolled across the tiles, making little clattering noises as they went. For a long moment Fran stared down at them, then slowly, reluctantly she looked up, to find the owner of that voice, a voice she remembered with a mind-spinning clarity.

'Surprised to see me?' Luke Calder said quietly.

'I. . . What do you want? What are you doing here?'

He pushed away from the wall where he had been lounging and advanced towards her, studying the shock on her face with mocking eyes. 'What do you think I'm doing here? We have some unfinished business, remember?'

Now that he had moved nearer Fran could see that there was a muscle ticking along the hard line of his jaw and that his eyes were glittering with something more than mere mockery, and she went cold. He wasn't just angry, he was furious, a cold, icy fury, which made answering shivers trickle along her spine. Never mind why he had come; this time he meant business!

She backed away, setting the width of the desk between them as she tried to work out what to say, although she doubted that he was in the mood to listen.

'Look, Mr Calder,' she began, 'I know you must be annoyed about what——'

'Annoyed! No, I'm not *annoyed*, Miss Williams. I'm furious.' He came right up to the desk, towering over her, despite the solid barrier of wood. He had shed the formal suit he'd worn previously and was dressed today in black trousers and leather jacket over a black silk shirt, sombre colours that only served to emphasise the olive cast of his skin, the night-darkness of his hair and eyes. He looked like the devil incarnate as he stood there glaring at her, and it took every scrap of courage and pride Fran possessed to stand and face him.

'All right then, Mr Calder, furious. But you must surely understand that I never meant things to get out of hand like that.'

'And is that supposed to make everything better? Come on, Miss Williams, you're not so naïve that you honestly believe that a mere apology will make up for the way you behaved.'

'The way *I* behaved? Now look here, I wasn't the one to blame for that ridiculous charade! That was your own fault for trying to make me get back into the car. If you'd done as I asked and left me alone then none of it would have happened.' Anger raced through her, warming away the coldness of shock. She glared back at him, feeling a momentary quiver when his jaw tightened even more, setting that betraying little muscle beating in a furious tempo.

'I asked—and I mean *asked*—you to get back into the car for you own safety. Have you no sense at all, can't you see how vulnerable you were, out in that street all by yourself? Damn it all, woman, I would have thought that talk you had in the car park with your two "friends" would have knocked some sense into your stubborn little head, but obviously it didn't!'

'Who are you calling stubborn? You were the one who refused to go away, the one who insisted on trailing me along the road. If you want someone to blame for what happened then try looking in the mirror, Mr Calder—then you'll see the culprit! Now, if you don't have anything more to say I suggest that you leave. I'm sure you can find your own way out.'

She sat down at the desk, pulling a sheaf of notes

towards her, her whole body trembling with tension as she felt Luke Calder watching her. She looked up, arching a brow as she said with false sweetness, 'Well, is there something else, then?'

He smiled, his narrow lips curling in a way that sent an immediate shiver of unease along her veins. 'There most certainly is. I'm afraid we haven't managed to clear up our little misunderstanding quite that easily. Do you remember the lady who rushed to your assistance last night and accused me of all those unspeakable designs on your virtue?'

'Yes.' Fran stared at him a puzzled frown marring her smooth brow.

'Well, it seems she wasn't too happy about the whole episode. So much so that she decided to call the police and give them my registration number, just in case I made a habit of kerb-crawling. I was awoken around seven this morning by two officers who spent the next hour cross-questioning me. Now can you understand why I'm neither ready nor willing to quietly let the matter drop?'

'I. . . I. . .it's unbelievable!'

'Unbelievable or not, it happened.'

'But didn't you tell them the truth? Surely they realised that it had all been a mistake once you explained?'

'The truth? That two hit men had waylaid you and that we were making our escape when you suddenly had a brainstorm and accused me of being in league with them? Do you really think they would have believed a story like that? This is rural England, Miss Williams, not the depths of downtown Chicago! If I'd told them a tale like that then they would have had me down at the station before I could blink!'

There was no doubting the anger in his deep voice as he roared at her, and in truth, Fran could understand it. If it hadn't been so awful it would have been almost comical, the thought that Luke Calder had been virtually accused of kerb-crawling!

'I'm sorry. You must understand that I never meant anything like this to happen. Last night I was upset. I said the first thing that came into my mind, but once I'd had time to think everything through I realised what a mistake I'd made. If there's any way I can make up for what's happened, Mr Calder, then I shall be only too pleased to do it.'

'Oh, there is—believe me, there is. And for starters you can get your bag and come with me.'

'Come with. . .? What do you mean? Where do you want me to go?'

'Down to the police station with me for a start, and then to visit that lady while we clear this whole mess up. You see, Miss Williams—or should I make that Fran, so that I can get used to calling you that?—I couldn't very well tell the police what had gone on last night, so I improvised. Now I need you to back up my story and put me in the clear. The last thing I need right now is a whole lot of unsavoury publicity if the Press gets hold of this tale.'

She wasn't going to like this, Fran had a deep-seated and inexplicable feeling, but she had to ask. 'And how, precisely, did you improvise? What did you tell the police, Mr Calder, if you didn't tell them the truth?'

He leant forward, resting his hands on the desk as he brought his face level with hers, his dark eyes glittering like jet. 'That what the old lady witnessed was nothing more than a lovers' quarrel.'

'What? Now look here, if you honestly think that I'm going down to the police station and verifying a story like that then you can think again! It's ridiculous. No one would believe it!'

'Oh, they will, they most definitely will, because you're going to make sure that they do.'

'And if I refuse?' Fran glared back at him, defiance in her eyes.

'Then very shortly you'll find yourself out of a job.' He stood up, his face betraying nothing but a ruthless determination. 'I expect you've heard rumours about the purpose-built radio station that's been planned. It's been on the drawing board for some time now but hasn't gone ahead because of lack of investment. When I was making my mind up about the new housing development I also looked into the possibility of putting some money into that project as well, to give me a bigger commitment in the area, which would help allay people's fears about it all being a get-rich-quick scheme. The more I put in then, logically, the more determined I'll be to see that it all goes through smoothly. I've decided to go ahead on both projects, Miss. . . Fran, which means that eventually I shall be a major shareholder in the station. It won't be difficult then for me to let it be known that I don't want you working here.'

'But that's blackmail! If I don't agree then I could find myself out of a job!'

'There's no "could" about it. Let me make myself very plain: I will not become the brunt of any unsavoury gossip and publicity. I've worked too damned hard to get where I am today to let it all be ruined by some silly, irresponsible female. Now if you're quite ready then I think it's time we went and put the record straight. And while we're at the police station I suggest that you have a word with someone there about the fact that you seem to be attracting some unwelcome attention. I saw your car in the car park when I arrived. Would I be wrong in thinking that your two visitors decided to leave their message in a more visible form?'

He was sharp, she had to hand him that—too sharp, in her estimation! How on earth had she ever got herself into such a mess? She should have refused to go with him last night and insisted on staying in the car park. It was doubtful if those two men could have done much worse than he was doing now! Lovers. . .she and Luke Calder? Never!

She stood up to walk stiffly around the desk, glaring at him as he stepped politely to one side and let her precede him from the room.

'Don't look so annoyed about all this, Fran. After all, you did have forewarning that it could happen.'

There was a cool mockery in his deep voice, and she turned to glare at him, hating him for the fact that he seemed to be deriving amusement from her discomfort.

'I have no idea what you mean. Frankly, if I'd had any forewarning of this then I'd have made certain that our paths would never cross again!'

'It might not have been as simple as that.' He caught her arm, stopping her when she would have carried on walking. Tilting her face with one long finger, Luke forced her to meet his eyes. 'Surely you remember what your researcher put in those notes, Fran? You must do. It made quite an impression on me. Capricorn and Virgo, destined to find attraction in each other. Our coming together as lovers, however temporary a state of affairs it may prove to be, was surely written in the stars!'

He was joking, deliberately using that cool mockery to pay her back. Yet, looking into those liquid dark eyes, Fran couldn't help the sudden feeling that she was standing on the verge of something so mind-blowing that it made her afraid.

She pulled away and walked ahead of him along the corridor, hearing the measured tread of his footsteps as he followed, and to her over-sensitive ears they seemed to match exactly the pounding, thudding beat of her heart.

'So that's it, Mr Calder, Miss Williams. You seem to have cleared this whole misunderstanding up quite satisfactorily. I'm sorry that you've both been troubled, but obviously you'll appreciate that we have to follow up any complaints of this nature.'

'Quite so, Sergeant. I'm only glad that we've been able to sort it all out so quickly. I have to admit that I was worried about anything being leaked to the papers,' Luke said.

'Oh, I don't think there's much danger of that, sir. No, I imagine this is the last you'll hear of the incident.'

'Well, that's a weight off our minds, isn't that right, darling?'

Luke Calder turned to shoot her a quick glance, and Fran did her best to paste a suitable expression to her face. Darling, indeed! 'Yes, it is. I hope we haven't caused you too much trouble, Sergeant,' she added politely.

'Not at all, madam. I only wish more complaints were as easily dealt with as this. Still, at least it's had a happy ending and brought you both together to make up your differences, and hopefully make you both think twice before starting another tiff in the future. These things have a habit of snowballing one way and another.'

Luke stood up, taking the policeman's hand and shaking it warmly. 'Thank you for your time, Sergeant. Right, if you're ready, darling, we may as well be on our way and pay our respects to the lady who made the complaint and set her mind at rest. Fortunately it doesn't look as if the sergeant is going to put me behind bars today!'

What a shame! thought Fran nastily as she stood up, holding herself rigid as she felt Luke Calder's arm slide behind her waist in a touching show of concern. Really, he was carrying this whole thing too far!

She left the interview-room, straining against the grip Luke kept on her waist as they walked out into the courtyard.

'I'm quite capable of walking unaided,' she snapped, glaring up at him.

'I'm sure you are, but, seeing that the sergeant is watching, we may as well finish this off properly for his benefit.' He helped her into the car, then raised a hand to the middle-aged policeman before sliding behind the wheel, the smile fading from his face.

'What's wrong?' Fran asked uneasily. 'The police seemed quite happy with the explanation we gave them.'

'I'm sure they were; however, if you think that's going to be the end of the matter then you're sadly mistaken.' He swung the car out of the yard while Fran stared at him in confusion.

'What do you mean?'

'Only that bad publicity has a nasty habit of surfacing, and that's the last thing I intend to let happen at this crucial stage.'

'I don't understand.'

'I'm sure you don't. Few people realise just how much depends on a man's reputation even in this day and age. This deal I'm involved in is a big one. You're not talking about a few thousand pounds but millions, millions I shall be borrowing from various banking concerns who are willing to lend that money on the strength of *my* reputation. Publicity like this from the gutter Press could ruin the whole deal.'

'Oh, surely not!'

'Surely yes! Banks are notoriously conservative about their dealings with clients. They won't be happy risking their money on a man who's been linked with kerb-crawling!'

'I think you're becoming hyper-sensitive. You heard what the sergeant said, that as far as he's concerned the whole incident can be dropped.'

'I heard, but I'm afraid it doesn't end there. What about this woman we're going to see? Can you imagine the damage she could do if she repeated her allegations around the town?' Luke glared at her, his dark brows lowered. 'That half-hearted performance you put on back at the police station won't be enough to convince her, not after what she witnessed last night. . .all your near-hysterical ramblings!'

Fran glared back at him. 'Well, excuse me! I did the best I could in the circumstances, Mr Calder, but you can hardly blame me if I find it difficult to appear besotted with your charms!'

'No? Then we shall have to find some way to make your next performance more convincing, won't we?' He slowed the car, turning it off the main road down a narrow lane that led to the river before bringing it to a halt and cutting the engine.

'What are you doing? I haven't got all day to waste. I have work to do.'

There was something about the expression on his face as he unclipped his seatbelt and turned towards her that made a sudden flurry of alarm run through her, and she backed as far away as the close confines of the car would allow.

'Neither have I any time to waste, so you must excuse me if I cut out the preliminaries.'

He reached across and unfastened her seatbelt, then pulled her to him, smiling tauntingly into her startled eyes before he bent and took her mouth in a kiss that sent a shaft of white-hot flame licking along her veins. Fran gasped, her whole body stiffening as wave after wave of heat enveloped her. She had been kissed before, but never had she felt this sudden flare of sensation, which stole her senses and made her pliant in Luke Calder's arms.

When his lips slid from her mouth to trail a fire-shower of kisses along the smooth line of her jaw she shuddered, her hands lifting to push him away before suddenly, helplessly sliding over the strong hard muscles of his shoulders to link behind his head. His dark hair was like cool, soft silk on her heated skin, and she slid her fingers into it, burying the tips deep in the silky strands, savouring the coolness. Deep down, in some tiny corner of her mind untouched by this scorching, debilitating heat, she knew this was madness, yet she seemed powerless to resist as his mouth moved back to hers, hot and urgent, seeking a response she had to give.

When abruptly he raised his head she shivered violently, instinctively moving closer to the source of the heat, her mouth lifting to his.

'Now that's better. I'm sure anyone looking at you now would be convinced that we're telling the truth. You really do look like a woman who's spent time making up with her lover now!'

The cool, tormenting mockery cut through the lingering haze of heat, sending ice into her veins. Fran drew back as though he had struck her, her face going pale as she saw the amusement on his face as he continued to study her.

'How could you?' she whispered hoarsely. 'What sort of a man are you, Luke Calder, to do that?'

He shrugged, turning the key in the ignition to start the car, his face in profile looking harsh and grim. 'You hardly need to ask me that. From what I saw the other day, you already have a full biography of me down to the very last detail, even though you'd missed one or two relevant facts. Now shall we get this over and done with? As you saw fit to remind me before, you do have work to do, the same as I have. And I've already wasted far too much time on you one way or another.'

He turned the car, his hands moving swiftly and expertly as he manoeuvred it in the narrow lane. He shot a quick look sideways at her before he headed back to the road. 'Don't look so upset. It was just a means to an end, that's all, not personal.'

'And that justifies everything, does it? That's the Luke Calder philosophy on life? To hell with anyone's feelings as long as you get what you want?' There was an icy contempt in her voice, and his face darkened in anger before he gave a faint dismissive shrug of his broad shoulders.

'It's a tough old world and I'd have thought you'd learned that lesson in your line of work. After all, you weren't overly concerned about my feelings when you interviewed me the other day, were you?'

'That was different! That was business.'

'And what do you think that was?' He laughed deeply, edging the car back into the traffic. 'I hate to disappoint you, Fran, but don't try reading anything into that kiss that wasn't there! To me it was business, nothing more, nothing less. Just a means to get what I want with the least amount of trouble.'

What could she say? How could she argue with someone who could be so cold-heartedly ruthless in his approach to life?

Fran sat back in the seat, staring unseeingly out of the window, wondering why she should feel the most ridiculous urge to cry at such evidence of Luke Calder's attitude to life. Of course, she could appreciate his fear of adverse publicity—she understood that only too well, thanks to what had happened to her father—but to employ such cold detachment in overcoming the problem it could cause was way beyond her understanding.

The house was only a few minutes' drive away from the river. Fran wished that it had been further away, wished that she'd had more time to compose herself and remove all traces of that kiss, but as she opened the door and got out of the car when they stopped in front of the neat little semi she was aware of the throbbing redness of her bruised lips, the faintly dishevelled state of her silvery hair.

She ran a shaking hand over the wispy tendrils, smoothing them back into the neat knot gathered at the nape of her neck, but without the aid of a comb or mirror it was impossible to return her hair to its usual immaculate style.

'You look fine. Stop fussing.' Luke came round the car and took her arm in a firm grasp to lead her through the gate and up the path to the front door.

Fran glared at him, pulling her arm sharply away. 'I look a mess and know I do! That was your whole idea.'

He smiled. 'You look exactly how you should, *darling*. Like a woman who's just been well and truly kissed. Now stop scowling and smile. The sooner this is sorted out then the sooner we can go our separate ways.'

'What a lovely thought! And stop calling me. . .' She broke off as the door opened, fixing a smile to her throbbing mouth as she recognised the elderly woman. 'I don't know if you remember me, Mrs Lewis. We met last night when you were walking your dog.'

'Of course I do! You're the young lady who was being. . . Oh!' The woman's face paled and she stepped back when she suddenly realised that Fran wasn't alone and who exactly it was with her. 'What do you want? I don't want any trouble!'

'It's all right, Mrs Lewis,' Fran said quickly. 'There's nothing at all to worry about. We just thought we'd better come and explain what had been going on last night.' She gave a tinkly little laugh, which sounded horribly false even to her own ears, and felt Luke Calder's fingers close around hers in silent warning.

'What Fran is trying to say, Mrs Lewis, is that what you witnessed last night wasn't quite what it appeared to be. Isn't that right, darling?' His voice dropped to a low note of affection as he slid an arm around her shoulders and drew her close to his side.

'Yes. Do. . .?' Fran swallowed hard, feeling the hard outline of his body pressing against the soft curve of her breast in a way that seemed to steal her breath. 'Do you think we could come in and explain? We won't take up too much of your time, but we really do want to clear up this misunderstanding.'

'Well. . . I suppose so.'

With marked reluctance, the elderly woman led them inside to a small sitting-room, which overlooked the garden at the rear of the house. 'Please sit down. This has all come as a bit of a shock. I didn't realise that you two knew each other, otherwise I would never have contacted the. . .' She broke off, colour running up her face as she pressed a guilty hand to her mouth.

Luke Calder sat down on the settee, pulling Fran down next to him as he favoured her with a smile that would have made a lesser woman fall in a grateful little heap at his feet. 'We know, don't we, my love? In fact, we've come straight round here from the police station. We spoke with a Sergeant Walker there. Please ring him if you feel you need to verify that fact.'

'I. . .' Obviously flustered, Mrs Lewis smiled shakily as she studied the cosy picture they made, sitting so close together on her sofa. 'That won't be necessary. If you'd just explain what was going on. I was so worried, you understand.'

'Of course you were. Any public-spirited citizen would have been. It must have looked very bad, but I'm afraid one doesn't always stop to think how a situation appears to an outsider.' Luke smiled again, reaching across the few inches of space Fran had managed to leave between them to catch her hand and raise it to his lips as he pressed a lovingly tender kiss to her fingertips. 'You must have had your fair share of lovers' tiffs over the years, Mrs Lewis, so I'm sure you understand how easily they can get out of hand.'

'So that's what it was!' The woman's face cleared like magic and she smiled back at him, not missing the subtle compliment he had paid her, and Fran had to bite back an urge to grind her teeth. The man was a master at manipulation, using that cold-hearted charm to ruthlessly convince the poor woman that this pack of lies was the truth!

'It was. I'm afraid Fran and I don't get enough time with each other because we're always so busy working, and that can lead to a lot of tension when we do meet. Last night it all seemed to flare up out of nothing.' Luke shrugged eloquently, his eyes like dark, dreamy pools of liquid as he favoured Fran with a lingering look before looking back at the older woman. 'And that's where you came in.'

'I feel such an old fool,' Mrs Lewis fluttered, smoothing the front of her cardigan. 'I should have realised that a lovely man like you would never have...' She turned to Fran, faint annoyance crossing her face. 'You should have explained what was going on.'

'I'm sorry.'

'Oh, you mustn't blame Fran. She was upset.' The words said one thing, but the tone of Luke's deep voice said entirely the opposite, and Fran shot him a withering look, then winced as his hand tightened around hers in a painful warning. 'Still, as long as we've managed to clear it all up now, it doesn't matter. You haven't mentioned what went on to anyone else, have you, Mrs Lewis?' He smiled slowly, his dark eyes alert and watchful. 'We'd feel such idiots if news of this leaked out.'

'Of course not, I. . .' She stopped abruptly, her face going red. 'Well, actually, that isn't quite true. Oh dear, if only you'd explained it all to me last night!' she said accusingly to Fran.

'Who else have you mentioned it to, then, apart from the police?' There was nothing in Luke's voice to suggest anything more than a mild curiosity, but Fran could feel the tension radiating from his powerful body as he leant forward in the seat. Suddenly she was filled with a strange sense of foreboding she couldn't understand.

'Just my nephew, Terry. I rang him to ask his advice, and he was the one who suggested I should contact the police. In fact, he made the initial call for me, as he has a lot of contacts at the station because of his job.'

Fran hardly dared ask, but that cold unease that was setting down roots forced her to. 'What sort of work does he do, Mrs Lewis?'

'He's a reporter, actually, on the local weekly paper. You might have heard of him: Terence Lewis?'

She'd heard of him all right. He was without doubt the very worst kind of news reporter, taking a few bare facts and embroidering them into a story! It was men like Terence Lewis who had spurred her on to get where she was today.

'Well, perhaps you can ring him after we've gone and explain that it's all been a mistake? We would like to put the record straight.'

There was no mistaking the grim displeasure in Luke's voice, and Mrs Lewis nodded nervously. 'Yes, of course I will. Right away, in fact, before he has a change to get started on that story.'

'Story?' The voice cracked like a whip now, and the woman jumped.

'He. . .he mentioned something about it being a scoop, that the man involved was someone well known . . .but, of course, he meant you!'

'So he knows who I am?'

'I'm afraid he must do. Someone at the station must have told him when they checked your registration. Oh, dear, oh, dear, this is all turning into a rather nasty mess, isn't it? You really *should* have explained what was going on,' she said, glaring at Fran.

'You should indeed, darling. That way you'd have saved everyone a whole lot of trouble.'

Fran didn't want to look at him, didn't want to turn her head and see the anger in those dark eyes, but there was no escaping the powerful force that drew her.

Just for a moment their eyes met and warred, then abruptly she turned away, feeling a river of ice sliding coldly along her veins. It was partly her own fault, of course. She should have followed her instincts and remembered what Debbie had written at the end of those notes, taken them as a warning and run as hard and as far as she could away from this Capricorn man!

CHAPTER FOUR

'WHY? Just tell me why it had to be me who was stupid enough to help you last night?'

Maybe it would have been easier if Luke had shouted and let loose the anger Fran could sense seething inside him, but he didn't. He just sat and stared at her, his face set, his eyes so cold that she shivered. Anything would have been better than this ice-cold contempt that cut her to the bone.

She looked away, taking a shaky little breath. 'I don't suppose it's any use saying that I'm sorry?'

'No use at all. Sorry isn't going to change anything, lady, as well you know. You're a reporter too, so you should know how their minds work!'

That stung, and she swung round in the seat, her hands clenching into fists. 'Don't you dare put me in the same bracket as Terry Lewis! I report the facts and stick to them. I don't go around making things up just to get myself a story!'

'So you keep on saying, but can you blame me for being sceptical when I recall the sort of facts you apparently deal with?' Luke's dark brows lowered and he leant forward to slip the key into the ignition and start the car with a throbbing roar of its powerful engine. 'To my mind you're all the same.'

'We're not!' Fran stopped, forcing the angry hysteria from her voice, realising it would do nothing to help convince him that he was wrong. 'Arguing isn't going to get us anywhere.'

'I agree. So what do you suggest?'

She shrugged. 'I don't really know. How about approaching Lewis and explaining the situation to him?'

'I don't think so.'

'Why not?'

'Because if he really is the sort of reporter you claim he is then that would be playing right into his hands by making him think I'm trying to hide something. What we need to do is steal his thunder in some way so that he realises how pointless it would be to write a story or even make any of those veiled suggestions that reporters of his ilk seem to be so good at.'

'We? I can't see that I'm involved in this any longer. I did as you asked and came to the police station and Mrs Lewis's, so that's where it ends, as far as I'm concerned.'

He flicked her a sideways glance, his mouth a thin line that sent fear tiptoeing along her spine. 'I'm afraid you're mistaken there. Until this whole ridiculous mess is sorted out you're involved right up to your pretty little neck. Don't forget what I warned you I'd do, and that hasn't changed. You either go along with me until this is over or you could soon find yourself out of a job, although I suppose you could always see if Lewis had an opening for you on his paper.'

'I'd rather starve first than work for a man like that!'

'Noble sentiments indeed, but you could find yourself changing your mind if you were pushed into that position. Still, there shouldn't be any need to let matters come to a head, not if you agree to be sensible and rectify your mistakes.'

'My mistakes! Oh, that's rich, really rich, blaming me!' She glared at him, but Luke appeared unconcerned as he turned the car into the car park, stopping next to where her car was waiting forlornly for the garage to collect it. Fran let her eyes linger on the scarred red paintwork and shattered windows of her little Fiesta, then looked away with a sigh. It really didn't seem fair that life should be throwing this at her all at once. One thing at a time she could have handled, but this. . .it was no wonder she suddenly felt that she didn't have the strength to carry on arguing.

'So what do you want me to do now?' she asked flatly.

'I'm glad you've decided to be sensible at last. It's really quite simple. All I intend to do is make sure that the story becomes public before Lewis can get it into print.'

'But I thought the whole idea was to keep it away from the public? Surely spreading it around will do the very thing you wanted to avoid by starting up all the rumours?'

Luke shook his head. 'Not if it's handled in the right way. We'll make a joke out of it, invite people to share our embarrassment. That way it will lose all its nasty overtones. We'll make certain that Lewis knows all the facts and can't twist them.'

'Facts? The real ones or that made-up version you concocted?' Fran demanded scornfully.

'The facts that we *were* quarrelling, that you *did* jump out of the car and refused to get back in when I tried to *persuade* you. The reasons behind all those *facts* are nobody's concern but ours.'

'And you really imagine that could do it?'

'Don't you? Lewis thinks he has a scoop, but once we let everyone know the truth then he'll have nothing left to play around with. End of story.'

It could work. Reporters like Terry Lewis needed so little to go on to formulate a story; he wouldn't even have to name Luke Calder, just make some veiled references to his identity that could be enough to discredit him. Hadn't much the same thing happened to her father, hints and innuendoes that had ruined his life? Fran couldn't in all conscience let it happen to Luke Calder now if there was a chance that she could help prevent it.

'All right, I suppose it's worth a try. What do you suggest we do?' she asked.

'Obviously we have to move fast, so I want you to accompany me to a dinner that the developers are giving tonight. There's bound to be Press coverage, and that means our friend Lewis should be there. It will be the ideal opportunity to put an end to this once and for all.'

'Oh, but isn't there some other way? I mean, tonight isn't all that convenient. I had something planned.' It was a lie; she had nothing planned apart from another glance through the news-cuttings. It was just the thought of having to spend more time in Luke Calder's company, which was more than she could face today.

'It isn't convenient for me to be the subject of a whole lot of unpleasant rumours! I've worked too damned hard just to let everything be ruined because of unsavoury gossip. If you have a date tonight then you're going to have to cancel it!'

His voice bit like a whip, and her face flooded with angry colour. 'I don't have a date! There's work I need to do.'

'Then I'm afraid it's going to have to wait. This takes priority over everything, as far as I'm concerned. Now, if you've finished making excuses then I have to go. I'll pick you up at seven.'

'There's no need to do that. I can meet you there.'

'No way. We're supposed to be a couple, not business acquaintances. I'll collect you and I'll take you home again afterwards, so save your breath and stop arguing.'

What could she say? Nothing. Fran nodded curtly, her lips compressed with anger as she thrust the car door open and got out.

'Oh, Fran. . .'

She paused in the middle of slamming the door, bending down to stare coldly at him. 'What?'

'Bearing in mind that this is supposed to be a social occasion, make sure that you dress accordingly and choose something suitable. . .something a woman would wear for a special night out with her lover.'

His audacity took her breath away. 'I don't think I need your advice on how to dress!'

'No?' Luke ran a swift look over her slender figure in the businesslike dark grey suit and white blouse. 'Appearances count for a great deal in this life, and if you appear tonight in an outfit like the ones you seem to favour then no one will believe our relationship is anything but a business one.'

'Don't worry, I'll do my level best to find something

more appropriate.' Fran smiled with a saccharin sweetness. 'You aren't the only one eager to get this cleared up!'

'I'm pleased to hear it. It's about time you realised how serious it all is and the intolerable position you've put me in with your irrational behaviour. I'll see you tonight.'

He revved the engine, and Fran stepped back and slammed the door with a touch more force than was really necessary, watching as he drove away without a backward glance. He really was the most annoying, irritating man she had ever met, and if it hadn't been for the fact that she knew he would carry out his threat and have her sacked she would have refused point-blank to go tonight. Twenty-four hours ago she had been barely aware of his existence; now he seemed to be taking over her life!

Would this do? Was this the sort of outfit a woman wore to meet her lover? It had been sheer vanity that had made Fran call at the exclusive boutique on the way home from work, and now as she studied the dress she wondered if that vanity had bordered on madness! She *never* wore clothes like this, so why had she succumbed to temptation? Because Luke Calder had made a few passing comments about her usual attire of pin-neat suits and blouses?

In a despairing sweep her gaze ran over the dress, and she bit back a groan. Why hadn't she realised in the shop just how the black silk clung, emphasising every slender curve? Even the tiny jet-buttoned bolero jacket looked less like a cover-up now than a blatant temptation, allowing the pearly sheen of her bare shoulders to gleam through the lace. She had washed and curled her silvery hair and left it long, brushing it so that it hung over one shoulder in a silky-pale swath, a style she never favoured. She looked exactly how she had wanted to look, like a woman who had dressed for a man, so why did she feel so unsure of herself now? Because that man was Luke Calder, that was why!

She spun away from the mirror and hurried downstairs, forcing the curling tension aside. This was a job, that was all, and if it entailed dressing in a way that she wouldn't normally do then so be it. It would be worth it just to get this whole silly mess sorted out.

She hurried into the living-room and went to the table to clear away the heap of news-cuttings. She had been working on them ever since she had got home, reading and re-reading the articles, but there was still no clue to unravel the mystery. Harry Martin maintained a high profile in the town, attending every major function, but there was little written about his business dealings. They seemed to be shrouded in mystery, and Fran was itching to find out more.

On the surface the man seemed to be part of the backbone of the community, but she had only to remember the marked reluctance shown by those of his employees she had tried to interview that afternoon to realise that all wasn't as it seemed. There had been genuine fear on some of those people's faces when she had mentioned Martin's name, a fear she could appreciate after what had happened to her last night, but it hadn't shaken her determination to get to the bottom of the story.

Gathering up the last of the cuttings, she locked them in her briefcase, then looked round, too restless and on edge to relax. There was still almost half an hour left before Luke Calder was due, time she would prefer to spend doing something to take her mind off the coming evening. In desperation she picked up the paper and turned to the TV guide, but there was nothing scheduled for the early-evening spot apart from game shows.

With a grimace she started to toss the paper down, then stopped when a column on the opposite page caught her attention. Rueing her own stupidity, yet somehow unable to stop herself, she ran a finger down until she came to her horoscope.

> Virgo: an unexpected outing could have far-reaching consequences, bringing romance into your life.

Her eyes widened and she stared at the page before throwing the paper down. Rubbish! Total and utter rubbish, written for the gullible. If she let herself believe even a word of that then she would be just as bad as they were!

The doorbell rang and she started violently before glancing at her watch with a frown. Surely this wasn't Luke so early?

She hurried to the front door, glaring at the man who stood on the step. 'You're early!'

'And good evening to you too. Is this your usual way of greeting your escorts? If so then it's hardly surprising you didn't have to cancel a date tonight.' He raised a mocking brow when she made no move to step aside. 'As you just pointed out so succinctly, I am early, so would you mind if I come in and wait?'

Fran stepped back, slamming the door before leading the way along the hall to the sitting-room with a marked ill-grace. 'Please yourself. I suppose I'd better offer you a drink now that you're here.'

'Ever the gracious hostess, I see,' he said with a cool irony, looking round the neatly furnished and immaculately tidy room with an expression on his face that irked her. 'Mmm...just how I imagined your home would look.'

Fran ignored the remark, terrified that the conversation could fast deteriorate into a verbal battle if she let it, although she would have dearly loved to know what he meant. 'What would you like?' she asked politely. 'Whiskey, gin?'

'Just tonic water, if you have it, please.' He prowled around the room, looking at the pictures, inspecting the books, seeming to dwarf the place with his large frame. She couldn't remember the last time that she'd invited a man into her home, and now it made her feel uneasy to watch Luke Calder inspecting all these snippets of her life. She wanted to snatch them up and hide them away from the coolly assessing scrutiny that seemed to lay her bare.

She drew in a quick little breath, forcing the ridiculous thought from her mind. 'I think I have a bottle in the kitchen. I'll just go and fetch it.'

Fran hurried from the room, then took her time filling the glass with tonic and adding ice cubes from the freezer, wanting to get back on to an even keel before she went back and faced him. What was it about him that seemed to knock her off balance this way, making her act so strangely out of character? He had only to appear and she could feel her emotions bubbling to the surface. Thank heavens that after tonight there should be no need for them to meet again.

She carried the glass back to the sitting-room, and came to an abrupt stop when she saw Luke standing by the window, reading the paper, which she'd left open at the horoscopes. He looked up when he heard her, and Fran felt a ripple of heat curl along her veins when she saw the smile curving his lips.

'I see you've been checking your horoscope.'

There was a wealth of meaning in his deep voice, and colour flared along her cheekbones. She glared at him as she set the glass down with a clatter. 'I was checking to see if there was anything worth watching on television.'

'So you haven't seen what the day has in store for you? Here, take a look. It makes interesting reading.'

He held the paper out to her, but she put her hands behind her back. 'No, thank you. I'm not interested in that. . .that rubbish!'

'So that's what you think it is? Then it won't worry you if I read it out to you, will it?'

'I'm not interested, Mr Calder! And you can't tell me that you believe all that mumbo-jumbo either!' She tried to inject scorn into her tone but had the idea it wasn't completely successful. There was something about the way he was watching her, his dark eyes so intent and. . .knowing, that fired her temper.

'I like to keep an open mind on most things, Fran, but if it upsets you then forget it. I just thought you might find it amusing.' He tossed the paper on to a chair, then picked up his glass and took a long swallow, watching her over the rim with open mockery.

'It doesn't upset me! Stop trying to put words into my mouth.' She drew in a quick breath, then let it out again in a rush. 'Look, I don't know what you're

playing at, but if you think you can foster some sort of
. . .ideas because of what you read the other day in my
notes then forget it. Our star signs have no bearing
whatsoever on how I feel about you!'

'And how *do* you feel about me?' He set the glass
down, taking a couple of slow, deliberate steps towards
her, his eyes pinned to her flushed face. 'This isn't
some sort of a confession, is it?'

'Confession?' Fran stared at him in confusion, feeling
a pulse starting to beat high in her throat as she met
the mesmerising stare.

'An admission that you're attracted to me?'

'Attracted. . .no!' She stepped back, colour swirling
under her skin. 'Don't be ridiculous!'

'No more ridiculous than what you just accused me of
trying to do.' His face hardened and he stared down at
her with contempt. 'When I want a woman, Fran, I don't
need to resort to auto-suggestion. The kind of woman
I'm interested in is adult enough to recognise what I want
from the outset. Now, if you're ready, we may as well
leave. The sooner this is over with the better.'

It was what she had thought only minutes before, so
why did she feel this strange little ache to hear him
repeat the sentiment? She picked up her bag and
followed him out to his car, hating him for making her
feel so gauche, and hating herself more for acting that
way in the first place.

Dusk was just falling as they turned into the parking
area down by the river. The dinner was being held on
a converted river boat, the *Gypsy Queen*, hired by the
developers for the evening. Fran had only been to the
luxurious floating restaurant a couple of times, but

knew from experience that the food was excellent and very expensive. Obviously no expense was being spared to make the night a success, and in different circumstances she would have been looking forward to it, but now, as silence settled over the car, she could feel herself growing tense.

She shot a quick look sideways, then visibly flinched when she found that Luke was watching her, with an expression of strained patience on his handsome face.

'All right, out with it. What's worrying you now?'

She barely spared him a glance, reaching for the door-handle. 'Nothing. Shall we go inside?'

She went to climb out, but he caught her arm and stopped her. Reaching across, he slammed the door again, then glared at her from the space of inches. 'Don't give me that! There's no way we're going in until you tell me what's wrong.'

'Nothing is wrong. Why should it be?' She smiled tightly, feeling the hot sting of tears behind her lids. Why was she acting like this? It shouldn't have mattered a jot what Luke thought of her, but it did.

He sighed impatiently, running a hand over his dark hair. He was wearing a dinner suit tonight, the fine black cloth fitting snugly across his wide shoulders and muscular chest, the thin lawn of his dress shirt gleaming white against the tanned smoothness of his freshly shaved skin. The formal clothes should have made him look more urbane and civilised, but they didn't. They only served to emphasise the power and toughness which was the man beneath the civilised veneer, and Fran shivered, wishing she had never started this by letting her emotions come to the surface.

'We seem to have got off on a wrong footing tonight,

Mr Calder,' she said carefully. 'I suggest that we try to put our differences aside for the next few hours and get on with the business at hand.'

'A truce? Is that what you're suggesting?'

She shrugged, not sure if she liked the sudden gleam in his dark eyes. 'If that's what you like to call it, yes . . .a truce.'

'And how long do you think it will last?'

'However long it needs to last. Why? Don't you think you can manage to stop needling me for a few hours?'

'Oh, I'm quite sure I can, but whether you can is another matter. Still, it's definitely worth a try, I expect.' He held his hand out. 'Shall we shake on it, then, Fran?'

She slid her fingers reluctantly into his, feeling the shudder that ran from the point of contact shooting up her arm in a most unsettling way. Quickly she pulled her hand away from his and opened the car door to scramble out. A cool little breeze was blowing, and she shivered as it ran playfully over her heated skin and ruffled the long strands of her silvery hair so that it spilled like spun gold down her back, tangling with the lace.

'Come along before you catch cold. You should have worn a coat over that dress—the night's not warm enough for an outfit like that.' Luke ran a swift glance over the fine open fabric covering her bare shoulders, and Fran fought against a desire to snap back an answer, and lost.

'I didn't have a coat I thought you would deem suitable. If you remember, you were quite specific in your requirements of what you wanted me to wear.'

'I remember, but that didn't mean I expected you to freeze to death.'

'Oh!' Enraged by such unappreciative comments after all the trouble she'd gone to, Fran swung round and marched ahead, stopping abruptly when she heard the unmistakable sound of his laughter.

'And what's so funny?'

'You are. Didn't you just agree to a truce? Well, by my reckonings it lasted, oh, all of three minutes. Is that a record for you?'

'Don't be smart! I never usually have any difficulty whatsoever holding on to my temper. It's just. . .' She broke off, suddenly wary of finishing the sentence.

'Just what?' Luke came closer, staring down into her widened eyes with a faint smile softening his face. 'Just that I seem to rub you up the wrong way? Was that what you were going to say?'

She shook her head. 'It doesn't matter. We'd better get inside.'

'And try to carry on with this truce?'

'Of course.' The breeze tossed her hair across her face and she reached up to smooth it back into place, feeling her pulse leaping when her fingers unexpectedly touched his. Very gently he caught the long glittering strands and brushed them behind her ear, his fingers lingering coolly against her flesh just for a moment before he let them drop to his side.

'It would be so much easier to maintain this truce if we were indifferent to each other, but we're far from that, aren't we, Fran?' He laughed softly, deeply, his eyes dark and full of secrets. 'Who knows what causes an attraction between a man and a woman? Maybe it does have something to do with the juxtaposition of the planets. It's as good a theory as any to explain it, because lord knows I never intended this to be anything other than a business arrangement.' He sighed with a wry self-mockery. 'Yet the last thing on my mind is business when I look at you in that witchy little dress!'

'I. . .' What could she say? Luke Calder might admit to a fleeting attraction for her, but she wasn't fool enough to think it was anything more than that. She knew what he was like, how he never did anything without having thought about the repercussions first. He would find it easy to allow that attraction to grow and take what he wanted from her, then cast her aside without a second thought. 'I'll take that as a compliment, Mr——'

He pressed a finger to her lips. 'Luke. Don't forget that for tonight at least you and I are meant to be lovers.'

Fran's pulse leapt and she stepped back at once, afraid that he would see the reaction his words evoked. Had he said that deliberately to unsettle her? Frankly, she wouldn't put it past him!

'Luke,' she repeated coolly. 'Just as long as you remember that this is all make-believe.'

He laughed softly, the wind catching the low rumble of sound and tossing it around so that for a moment the very air seemed to be filled with it. 'Would I ever do such a thing, Fran?'

She glared at him, her eyes flashing as she felt the lingering shudder of sensation rippling across her skin. 'If it served your purpose then yes, you would! Don't forget that I know exactly what you're capable of!'

'Guesswork. . .or an observation founded on all those facts your researcher dug out for you? What did it say in those notes? Ah, yes, that's it: ambitious, calculating, even ruthless. You surely don't believe any of that, do you? You can't do, not when you've been at pains to tell me what rubbish all this astrological mumbo-jumbo is. But if you do believe it then you must also believe the rest of it and realise that our relationship is destined to move along quite different channels than purely business ones.'

'I... I... Ohh!' She swung round and marched along the path to where the boat was moored, and this time didn't make the mistake of turning back when she heard him laugh.

CHAPTER FIVE

'IT's the last time we'll have an argument in the middle of the street, I can tell you. We can laugh about it now, can't we, darling? But it wasn't funny this morning when the police arrived on the doorstep. I'm only glad that we'd made up, otherwise it could have been very awkward for me if Fran had refused to back up my story!'

The group clustered around them laughed in appreciation before the conversation drifted along more general channels. Fran had to hand it to Luke: he had handled the story with a panache that must have squashed any rumours stone-dead. She glanced round, spotting Terry Lewis on the outer fringes of their circle, an expression of chagrin on his face. He had obviously heard every word, and from the look of it was none too pleased to have a juicy story snatched from under his nose.

'Well, do you think that did it?' Under cover of the conversation, Luke drew her attention, his hand brushing against her arm through the fine fabric of the lacy jacket, and she started nervously so that a few drops of wine spilled over the rim of her glass. Hurriedly she licked them from her fingers, then looked up and felt her pulse jerk when she saw the way he was looking at her mouth.

'Yes, I'm sure it will be fine now. Lew... Lewis

seems to have got the message, so I doubt if he'll try to make a story out of it.'

She sounded breathless and he frowned, his eyes lifting to hers for a moment before someone drew his attention and he turned away. Fran set her glass down, murmuring an apology as she made her way through the crowd and out on to the deck. She walked over to the rail and leant her forearms on it as she stared across the river, and drew in a shuddery little breath, hating the fact that Luke could make her so aware of him with just a look.

'So, how long have you and Calder known one another, then?'

She jumped violently, swinging round, glad of the darkness that hid the shock in her eyes when she saw that Terry Lewis had followed her and was standing just a few feet away.

'Some time. Why? What interest is it to you?' There was a barely veiled hostility in her tone, and she caught herself up short. Lewis was a professional, and although she might not agree with his methods she had to face the fact that he would quickly sense something was wrong unless she was very careful. Luke would never forgive her if she gave them away with some unwitting comment.

'Anything that happens in this town is of interest to me, as it is to you, being in the business of reporting what goes on yourself.' He moved closer, delving in the pocket of his dinner jacket to lift out a carton of cigarettes and light one, his pale eyes gleaming as he studied her over the glowing tip. 'You managed to keep the news of your relationship very secret, Fran. It makes me wonder just how long it's been going on, or if it was merely a way to get Calder out of an awkward situation.'

Fran laughed, forcing a light amusement to her voice. 'Why should you think that? Come on, Terry, even you can't be so desperate for a story that you'd try to make something out of last night's little mishap! What are you trying to say...that I wasn't the woman involved? I think your aunt can vouch for the fact that I was.'

He turned and leant against the rail, drawing deeply on the cigarette before letting the smoke drift away on the night's breeze. He was a good-looking man in his late thirties, and Fran had met him on several occasions but had never liked him, finding something faintly repugnant about the way he stood on the outside of life looking in, searching for anything unsavoury. Terry Lewis was a voyeur, an observer of life who never committed himself to becoming part of it. Other people's tragedies and sorrows were to him just good copy.

'I'm sure she can. She phoned and told me about your visit this afternoon; however, I shall reserve the right to be sceptical a while longer. I heard your interview with Calder yesterday, you see, and it didn't strike me that you two were...close.'

Fran shrugged, turning her face away from his calculating scrutiny, studying the way the moonlight bounced and sparkled off the water with a fixed expression on her face. 'My feelings for Luke have no bearing whatsoever on how I interviewed him. That was strictly business as far as I was concerned.'

'So you're saying that you're able to detach any personal feelings from any professional ones?' He smiled, taking a last draw on the cigarette before tossing it over the rail. 'I'm full of admiration for your single-mindedness, Fran. In my experience, very few women can remain detached, but you must be one of that rare breed, because I formed the distinct impression that you didn't even like Calder when I heard you interviewing him, but how wrong can one be?'

He didn't believe her, Fran could tell, and she hurried to convince him. 'Just because Luke and I share a close personal relationship it doesn't mean that we agree on everything. I have my own views on the development, and obviously they showed!'

'They did indeed. I've rarely heard a more entertaining interview. It's no wonder you were quarrelling last night—he had you backed into a corner a couple of times with facts you didn't know. Still, I suppose you would have to develop a certain detachment, otherwise you'd never be able to carry on with what you're working on at the moment.'

'What I'm working on? Sorry, Terry, but you've lost me there.'

'Harry Martin...the word's out that you're interested in how he conducts his business at the moment, and of course that must cause untold problems, or would do if you weren't able to separate your professional and personal life.'

It startled her that he should know this much when she had tried so hard to be circumspect in making her enquiries. 'I don't know what you're talking about,' she said evasively. 'Why should I be interested in Martin?'

'I have no idea as yet, but rumour has it that you are. It must put you in something of a dilemma, knowing that your boyfriend is rather heavily involved with him.'

'What? Are you telling me that Luke and Harry Martin are in business together?'

'You didn't know? Seems that you aren't the only one to keep your business life and your personal one separate. You two must be better matched than I thought.'

His pale eyes glittered spitefully as he smiled at her before walking back inside. Fran leant heavily on the rail, feeling cold tentacles of shock closing around her heart. Had he been telling the truth? Was Luke working with Harry Martin? Every bit of her shied away from the idea, but what had Terry Lewis to gain from lying when she could find out the truth?

'There you are! I was wondering where you'd disappeared to. What did Lewis want? Was he trying to quiz you about last night?'

Her pulse leapt at the sound of Luke's voice and she turned around, searching his face. How much had he heard of that conversation? Suddenly, for some inexplicable reason, it seemed important that he shouldn't have heard what Terry Lewis had just said.

'I think he was sceptical about our story but has accepted that it would be a waste of time trying to make anything out of it now.'

'Too damned right it would! I wondered what he was up to when I spotted him coming back inside while I was looking for you.' Luke moved closer, his arm brushing hers as he leant against the rail, one eyebrow quirking when she immediately moved away. 'You're very nervous, Fran. Does it always bother you when a man comes within touching distance, or is it just the effect I have on you that makes you flinch away?'

'Don't flatter yourself! Now, if you came out here to annoy me then. . .'

'I came out here because people were starting to ask where you were. I think they found it surprising, after all the trouble we've gone to to promote this loving relationship, that you've strayed so long from my side.' He turned slightly, the pale silvery light casting deep shadows on his strongly carved features. 'Surely you don't want to ruin all our good work, do you, darling? It would mean that we'd have to continue this charade in the future.'

'Don't darling me! And if you think for a single moment that there's going to be a repeat of tonight then think again. I've repaid my debt, and that's it as far as I'm concerned!'

She glared at him, hating the treacherous little ache in her heart at the thought that he might be in league with Harry Martin.

'Not quite. There's still an hour or so to go before we're due to dock. An hour that I intend to use making sure that everyone, including your friend Lewis, understands what our relationship is! Now, if you're quite ready, shall we go back inside?'

He held his hand out to her, but Fran ignored it, brushing past him to head towards the door leading back from the deck. Suddenly the boat dipped as it hit a swell and she staggered, cannoning heavily against Luke before reeling towards the rail.

'Careful!' He grasped her around the waist, his hands warm and hard through the thin silk of her dress as he steadied her, and Fran felt her heart run wild. Just for a moment she looked up and her eyes met his, wide, unguarded, and she felt his fingers tighten.

'Fran.' Her name was a mere whisper of sound, soft, hauntingly beautiful, said that way in that slow deep voice with its touch of Scottish burr, and she shuddered helplessly, feeling the echoes rippling through her, making her go weak with a hot longing she barely understood and couldn't hope to fight. When he slowly drew her to him she made no attempt to struggle, held by the soft beauty of that one word and the warm security of his hands at her waist. He brought her close against him, his arms enfolding her slenderness against the hardness of his powerful body for a long quiet moment before he slid his hand beneath her chin and lifted her face to his.

There was an instant when she sensed him hesitating, as though giving her time to draw away, but that was the last thing on her mind as she stared into the glittering warmth of his eyes.

Driven by a need she had never felt before, she pressed herself closer, her lips parting in an unconscious invitation, and heard the rough, wildly exciting groan Luke gave before he took her mouth in a kiss that burned with a raw fire. Time after time his lips swept over hers before his tongue slid inside her mouth to tangle with hers in a rhythm that sent a frenzy of red-hot sensation along her veins. The breeze flowing off the river was cool, but it couldn't cool the hot flames of desire she could feel curling inside her.

When he drew back to skim a line of kisses down the slender column of her neck to where a pulse was beating in a frenzied rhythm she moaned softly, glorying in the feel of his mouth on her skin. Her hands slid up, her fingers running along the strong line of his throat to caress the faintly rough skin along his jaw, her fingertips burning at the contact.

'Fran!' This time there was no softness in the sound, no gentleness, just a raw aching need for possession, which she immediately recognised and gloried in.

In a slow seductive sweep her hand continued its caress, moving delicately across the angular plane of his cheek to trace the curve of his ear, the silkiness of the hair at his temples. A shudder ran through him at the touch of her fingers and he drew her closer, crushing her against the powerful length of his body so that she could feel his heart thundering against her breast.

The sound of the door opening and of voices as people came out on to the deck shocked her so much that she felt physically sick. Just for a second longer she stayed in Luke's arms, her whole body trembling, before abruptly she moved away and walked over to the rail.

'Fran.'

She didn't want to hear what he would say, didn't want to compound this foolishness with more folly, didn't want to hear him gloat at her easy capitulation. Why had she allowed herself to respond like that, invited him to kiss her that way? She felt the sickness growing, welling hard and hot in her stomach, but not hot enough to completely burn away the lingering echoes of passion, and she was filled with shame.

'Was that all part of the plan too?' she asked brittly, forcing herself to turn and look at him, to face what she had done. 'I really should try to remember how your mind works. Did you plan that little interlude before you came looking for me, just as you planned what happened this afternoon?'

He seemed to hesitate, his face partly shadowed as the moon slid silently behind a cloud, leaving the boat in darkness, yet Fran could sense him studying the bruised swell of her lips, the faint tremble coursing through her body. When he lifted his hand she shrank back, terrified that he would touch her again, but all he did was push the heavy dark hair back from his forehead, his voice coolly impersonal when he answered, 'I always find it useful to make plans.'

She shouldn't have felt this sense of grief, shouldn't have felt *betrayed*, but she did. Coldness ran through her, turning her limbs to ice, her aching heart to stone. All that was left to her now was to not let him know just how much he had hurt her.

'Well, may I suggest that the next time you make your plans you leave me out of them? Not even my job is worth having to go through a repeat of that!'

She started past him, but he caught her arm, his fingers biting into her flesh through the fine fabric. 'I didn't notice it being a case of your putting up with anything! You were with me every step of the way in that kiss.'

She jerked her arm away, rubbing the bruised flesh, her eyes spitting back at him like a cornered animal. 'With you or ahead of you, Mr Calder? You aren't the only one who can make plans, you know.'

'Meaning?' he said softly, but she wasn't fool enough to miss the anger beneath the seemingly mild question. He didn't like having the tables turned on him, didn't like being the one on the receiving end.

'Meaning that I let you kiss me once I realised that

was your intention, because I too thought that it would serve a purpose and stop Terry Lewis making any more waves. Did you think I was actually enjoying it?' She laughed, a bitter amusement in her voice. 'I must be a better actress than I imagined! Still, at least if Lewis was watching us it should have done the trick. If it fooled you and you were—how shall I put it?—intimately involved then it most certainly would have fooled him!'

Fran smiled sweetly up at him, feeling the tears flowing, unseen, in her heart. 'Now shall we go back inside and carry on with our little game of make-believe? It seems a pity to waste all our hard work.' She reached up, feeling him flinch as she ran her finger lightly over the chiselled perfection of his upper lip to wipe away an imaginary trace of lipstick. 'There, that's better. We don't want to overdo the acting, do we?'

'Make-believe, was it, Fran?' His voice was still soft, but there was no trace of anger now, just a faint amusement, which for some strange reason frightened her even more. When he moved to stand in front of her, barring her path, she looked down, terrified that he would read her fear on her face.

'I've just said it was,' she said shortly.

Luke laughed, reaching out to tilt her chin and look into her eyes with an expression on his face that made an immediate shudder run down her spine. 'Then all I can say is that if that was make-believe I can't wait to sample the real thing!'

'I. . .you. . .' There had to be something she could say, something sharp and snappy, tailor-made to disabuse him of that idea, but wasn't it just typical that she couldn't for the life of her think what it was?

* * * *

It was nearer two hours than one before they got away. After the boat returned to its moorings people seemed reluctant to break up the party. Finally Fran led the way down the gangplank, feeling waves of tiredness washing over her. The whole night had been a strain, and now all she wanted was to get away from the throng, and, more importantly, away from Luke.

He unlocked the car door, holding it for her while she slipped inside with a quiet murmur of thanks. He had been nothing other than polite since that confrontation they had had on the deck, maintaining the charade of their relationship with apparent ease, yet Fran had sensed the tension behind the smiling façade. He might have had the last word, but he hadn't really forgiven her for her temerity in trying to put him down. Did he see it as some kind of a challenge? She sincerely hoped not! Luke Calder was used to getting what he wanted from life, and the last thing she needed was for him to turn his sights on to her, even though it might only be to put her back in her place!

'Tired?'

Fran brought her thoughts back to the moment, forcing a slight, polite smile to her lips as she flicked him a quick sideways glance. 'A bit. How about you?'

He shrugged, backing the car out of the parking space to turn it deftly up the narrow unpaved path leading up from the river. 'About the same. More relieved that it's over, probably.'

She rested her head back against the soft leather seat, watching the patterns formed by the trees against the night sky as they drove steadily back to the road. 'So you're more or less convinced that we pulled it off?'

'Oh, yes. I have no doubts on that score. Didn't you hear a couple of the men warning me to be careful on the way home and not start any arguments with you?' Luke laughed shortly. 'Seems that everyone appreciated the joke and took it exactly as we intended them to, even your friend Lewis in the end.'

She flicked him an irritated glance. 'I wish you wouldn't call him that. He's no friend of mine!'

'No? You two looked very cosy, chatting away out on the deck. Sure you weren't plotting something together, being kindred spirits, so to speak?'

'No, we weren't, and I thought you said you saw Lewis as he came back inside after talking to me? You never mentioned that you were watching us.' Fran sat up straighter, feeling the flurry of unease that ran along her spine as once again she wondered what Luke had overheard of that conversation. All night long the thought of his being hand in glove with Harry Martin had lingered at the back of her mind. It would be easy enough to ask him straight if there was any truth in it, so why didn't she just come on out and ask? Because she didn't want to hear that it was true!

'I wasn't *watching* you. I just caught a glimpse of you both through one of the windows, but Lewis had already started to come back inside when I went out there to fetch you back.' His face tightened and he shot her a quick assessing glance. 'Why do I get the distinct impression that you sounded on the defensive, then? Were you plotting something, Fran?' His voice dropped lower, taking on a steely edge that cut through the air. 'I think I should warn you that it would be a mistake to underestimate what I'm capable of. I make a bad enemy, Fran, a very bad one indeed!'

'Don't be ridiculous! You're getting paranoid, that's your trouble. I wasn't plotting anything at all. Frankly, after tonight is over and done with you and I will never meet again, thank heavens!'

'You sound very sure of that, but how can you be?'

'Of course I am. I agreed to help you out tonight, but that was all I agreed to. From now on you're on your own!'

'And what about fate, destiny, or whatever else you like to call it? Remember your notes, Fran, and what they said about us being so perfectly compatible. Surely no power on earth or celestial is going to just let us drift apart?'

He was deliberately taunting her and she knew it. So why did she find it so difficult to ignore the mocking, taunting comments and treat them with the silent scorn they so richly deserved?

'Rubbish! Even if there is anything in all this astrological nonsense then you have to view it in context. I can't be the only Virgo you'll meet in your entire life! Lord knows what the percentages are, but there must be millions of us about!'

'I'm sure there are, but I can quite honestly say that you're the first one I've been aware of, or who's made such a marked impression on me after so short an acquaintance.' Luke shook his head, his mouth curled into the kind of annoying smile that made her fingers itch to slap it away. 'I think that you and I are destined to continue this very special relationship whether we like it or not.'

'Do you, indeed? Then I'm afraid you're going to be sadly disappointed.' She glared at him, waiting until he had stopped the car outside her house before treating him to a cold smile. 'Right, this is it, then, the end of our forced alliance. I can't honestly say that it's been a pleasure, but it has been an experience...one I most definitely don't want to repeat!'

'And what happens when people start asking about you, wondering why we aren't together?' He turned slightly in the seat, the light from a street-lamp gilding the carved tanned planes of his face, turning the thickness of his hair to midnight silk, so that despite herself Fran felt a tiny ripple of appreciation for his male beauty. He really was a most exceptionally handsome man, but she knew from experience that it was all on the surface. Underneath, Luke Calder was as tough and hard as old nails.

'I'm sure you'll manage to come up with something plausible. Why don't you make a few plans, get your tale all neatly worked out in advance, the way you do with everything?' Fran slipped the catch on the door, then paused, holding her hand out to him, determined to let him know that this was the finish of their "relationship". 'I think we're just about quits now, don't you? So let's shake on it.'

Luke took her hand, but instead of shaking it lifted it to his mouth and turned it over to press his lips to the very centre of her palm, watching the shock that widened her grey eyes at the tingling contact. Slowly he removed his mouth, closing her fingers over the spot where his lips had left a burning imprint, a brand on her flesh.

'I think we've passed the point of shaking hands, Fran, don't you?'

For a moment that bordered on eternity, Fran stared at the throbbing centre of her hand, then snatched it away and scrambled from the car, uncaring what interpretation he put on her haste. She'd had enough today, and now all she wanted was to get inside and lock the door on Luke Calder and all the problems he kept bringing into her life. But instead of peace and solitude and a chance to get her emotions under control, she opened the door and found herself in the middle of a nightmare.

Broken glass and china lay everywhere, littered across the torn remains of the carpet which had been ripped from the stairs. There wasn't an inch of clear floor anywhere, so that she could hear the sickening crunch of glass under her feet as she made her way along the hall and peered into the sitting-room, to be met by a scene of similar devastation. It was a scene straight out of one's worst nightmares, and she had to clutch hold of the door as shock took the strength from her limbs.

'What the. . .? Fran. . . Fran! Where are you? Damn it. . .answer me!'

She felt no surprise at hearing Luke's voice—indeed, she felt nothing but a cold numbness as she stared round at the ruins of her home. When he came and laid his hand on her shoulder she didn't move, just stared blankly up at him, her face the exact colour of the torn paper strewn across the floor. He swore softly, colourfully, his face like granite as he swept a gaze round the room before lifting her into his arms and carrying her from the house. He set her down beside the car, his arm firm around her shoulders as he steadied her and opened the door to put her gently inside.

Bending down, he stared into her face, his long

fingers strangely gentle as he cupped her cheek and made her look at him. 'Stay there, Fran. Understand? Just stay there in the car and leave this to me.'

There was such quiet authority in his deep voice that she nodded, instinctively obeying the command, remaining stiff and unfeeling as she watched him go back inside. Lights flared as he moved from room to room, obviously checking the rest of the house. When he came back out again there was a grim anger in his face as he strode back to the car and climbed in beside her. 'I've phoned the police. They should be here soon. We'll wait out here for them.'

He glanced quickly at her, his eyes darkening when she merely nodded like an obedient puppet. Reaching across, he drew her into his arms, settling her head against his shoulder as he stroked her ice-cold cheek with a gentle hand. 'It'll be all right, Fran. Don't worry, I'll sort it all out for you.'

The tenderness in his deep voice was her undoing, breaking the wall of her composure. She gave a tiny strangled gasp and shuddered, feeling the waves of shock coursing along her veins. 'Luke, I. . .'

'Shh! Don't try to talk. You've had a shock. Just take it easy for a few minutes and save your strength for when the police arrive. God, if I could just get my hands on the bastards who did that to your house! Let's just hope the police find out who's responsible, Fran.'

They wouldn't find out. Even though she had only had time to glimpse the devastation that had been wrought, she knew that it had been a professional job, carried out by men who would leave no trace behind them. There would be no clues, no fingerprints, nothing to lead the police to them, but she knew who they were, just as she had known last night who had wrecked her car. Harry Martin was behind all this, and, although she hadn't a hope of proving it, she knew it for a fact.

She drew away from him, moving to the very edge of the seat, cursing Terry Lewis for planting the seeds of suspicion in her head. It would have been so good to just sit there and let Luke hold her, to draw comfort from his strength, but how could she do that when he was supposedly in league with the man who had done that to her house? She had told no one that she would be out for the whole night; the only person who had known had been Luke Calder. Had he told Martin? She had to face the fact that it could be so.

'I'm going back inside,' she said. 'Don't worry, I'm not about to collapse at your feet. You don't have to stay. I'll be quite all right.'

'Maybe I don't have to, but I have every intention of doing so. What kind of a heel do you think I am, Fran, that I'd drive off and leave you here on your own?'

There was a thread of anger in the question, but Fran ignored it, just as she forced herself to ignore the sudden surge of hope that filled her heart. She mustn't allow herself to be swayed by emotion. She had to look at the facts and analyse them, then draw the right conclusions. She already knew how important business was to Luke, that it was the single driving force in his life. She couldn't be foolish enough to ignore the fact that he had already stated that he would go to any lengths to protect it.

'Stay if you want to, then. I'll be glad of the company, I expect, while I'm waiting for the police. Shall we go inside?' She arched a brow at him, feeling a shudder of pure sensation when she saw the open admiration in his dark eyes.

'You're a whole lot tougher than you look, Fran. Most women would have gone to pieces, coming back to find this.'

Tough? No, she wasn't tough. She couldn't be. Someone who was tough wouldn't be feeling this horrible nagging ache deep in her heart. But she had spent the whole long night playing at make-believe, so surely she could manage to play the game a while longer.

CHAPTER SIX

THE police came, brusquely sympathetic as they assessed the damage and then informed Fran that there would be men sent out to dust for fingerprints the following day. It was obvious that they, too, had realised what a professional job it was, something reflected in their searching questions as to whether she thought she had any enemies.

Reluctant to voice her suspicions, Fran skirted round the answers, aware that Luke was listening intently to every word she said.

He was far too sharp to miss how evasive she was being, and she knew that once the police had left there would be more questions to answer; however, that was the least of her concerns. The fact that Harry Martin had seen fit to go this far not only alarmed her but also made her realise that she must be on to something. The question, of course, was, what?

The police finally left after advising her not to touch anything until the fingerprint team had been. Fran closed the door and stood silently looking at the mess. It was going to take days to get everything sorted out, and she suddenly felt quite unable to cope with it all.

'Are you all right?' Luke came into the hall, his hands pushed into the pockets of his trousers, his bow tie hanging loose around his neck, seemingly relaxed, but she could sense the leashed tension in him and forced a shaky smile, wanting to avoid a confrontation just yet. 'Yes. I was just wondering where to start.'

She looked round the hall, then bent to pick up the broken remains of a photo frame.

Shaking the loose shards of glass from the splintered frame, she stared down at the dearly familiar face of her father, and felt some of the waning strength flow back to her limbs.

This had been a cruel blow, but it wouldn't stop her from ensuring that justice was done.

She owed it to the town, and she owed it to the memory of Frank Williams, her father, who'd had no one to fight for him when he'd needed it most.

'Who did this, Fran? No, don't try being evasive with me the way you were with the police, because it won't wash. You *know* who's responsible for this, just as you knew who'd sent those men, and wrecked your car last night. And I don't think that it's too far-fetched to assume that person is one and the same!'

There was a harshness on his face as he moved towards her, a determination to make her tell him the answers he sought, and she looked away. 'I don't know what you mean,' she said shortly. 'I've no more idea of who did this than the police apparently have.'

'No?' Luke smiled tightly. 'You're a poor liar, Fran, and you know it. That's why you can't look me in the eyes.' He tilted her chin, his fingers firm against her flesh. 'So try again, and this time make it the truth. Only then will I be able to help you get out of this mess you seem to have got yourself into.'

His arrogance took her breath away, and she jerked her head back. 'You can help me? And what makes you think you can do that? How do you intend to deal with the kind of mentality that ordered this?' She swept a hand round the wrecked hallway, then looked back at him, feeling suddenly sick with suspicion. 'Unless you know more about it than you're admitting to.'

'I beg your pardon?' There was no mistaking the sudden anger in his deep voice, and despite herself Fran took a step back, feeling a tiny tremor running through her limbs. 'Are you accusing me of being involved with the people who did this...are you?' He reached out, catching her by the shoulders to jerk her back towards him and give her a hard shake that made her head spin.

'I...' Fran swallowed down the cold chill of fear in the pit of her stomach, the bile of suspicion. She didn't want Luke to be involved, but she couldn't help but remember what had been said.

'Answer me! You can't just accuse me without backing that accusation up. So tell me why you think I'd want to wreck your home? What would I stand to gain from such an act of mindless vandalism?'

'I don't know! I don't know what to think any more, don't you understand?' Tears misted her eyes as she stared back at him, wishing she didn't feel so confused, and heard him curse softly, as though the words were torn from him against his will. He pulled her into his arms, running a hand up and down her spine to soothe away the tension.

'All right, all right. Let's drop it for now. Don't upset yourself. This must have been one hell of a shock, and you're overwrought, that's all. Just believe me when I say that I had nothing whatsoever to do with any of this. So whatever crazy thoughts you're harbouring, forget them!'

'Yes.' She wanted to believe him, wanted to believe that note of compassion in his voice was real so much that it hurt. After all, she had nothing to go on apart from what Terry Lewis had told her, and she knew what a liar he was.

'What you need is some rest,' said Luke. 'You're totally exhausted. Once you've had time to sleep you'll feel better able to cope. I can arrange to have someone come in and clear up this mess in the morning after the fingerprint team have finished.'

'Oh, but I can't let you do that,' she protested, pulling out of the warm security of his arms. 'This isn't your problem, Luke.'

'I disagree. If you hadn't accompanied me tonight then none of this might have happened. I'll get it sorted out just as soon as I can. Now let's get out of here.'

'Out? But where are we going?'

'You can't stay here, Fran. You need to get some rest, but you can't use any of the bedrooms, not with the state they're in. I'm going to take you back with me.'

'Oh, but I——'

'No buts.' He smiled to soften the order, but there was no mistaking the glint of determination in his dark eyes as he held her firmly in front of him. 'I won't take no for an answer. I'm not leaving you here all alone, so it's a case of you either coming with me, or of me staying here for the rest of the night and neither of us getting any rest. Make up your mind which it's to be, Fran.'

'I. . . Oh. . .but. . .' There was no doubting that he meant what he said, and she glared at him, realising that she was beaten. Which was worse—staying here for the night or going back with him to the hotel? At least there she would have the privacy of her own room and the security of other people around.

'I suppose I shall have to come with you, if you're sure that the hotel will have a free room.'

'I'm quite certain there won't be a problem. Now come along.'

'But won't I need to pack a bag? I can't just arrive like this, with nothing.'

His face tightened into a grim mask and he cast a hard look up the stairs. 'I doubt if you'll find anything to pack. Most of your clothes seem to have suffered the same fate as the rest of your belongings, Fran. You're going to have to replace them.'

'Oh, I see.' There was a lost note in her voice, and he sighed roughly, impatiently.

'Why won't you tell me who's responsible for all this? Dammit, woman, if they'd do something like this then there's no knowing what they'll do next!'

She wanted to tell him, wanted to share it with him and have him sort it out, lean on the strength of Luke Calder, but that tiny seed of suspicion held her back. Until she could prove without the shadow of a doubt that he wasn't in league with Harry Martin then she couldn't risk doing that, no matter how she might long to.

'There's nothing to tell. You heard the police: this was a professional job. They don't think they'll find whoever is responsible, so how can I hope to?' Fran turned to leave, then stopped to pick up the photograph of her father. She would take it with her, use it as a charm to stop herself weakening in her resolve to uncover the truth, even though it might be unpalatable.

She glanced at Luke, studying the set of his tall body, the lean planes of his face, and felt her heart contract.

Please heaven that she wouldn't find out that he was involved after all, because something warned her that that would be more than she could ever cope with.

'Here? But that can't be right! You were staying at the Imperial when I phoned you to set up the interview last week. What do you mean, you're staying here?' Fran turned and glared at Luke, feeling her heart thudding painfully when he smiled with an easy charm that sent little tingles shooting down her spine.

'I left the hotel a couple of days ago. I was lucky enough to be offered this house to rent, so I jumped at the chance. I hate staying in hotels, they're so impersonal, and this is rather spectacular. Don't you agree?'

He looked calmly through the windscreen, his face betraying nothing but admiration as he studied the elegant lines of the ultra-modern split-level house standing on the banks of the river, but Fran wasn't fooled. He had tricked her, deliberately let her think that they would be going back to the hotel, but if he thought she was going to meekly go along with his conniving then he was going to be sadly disappointed.

'Well, I'm not staying here! Don't think you're going to get away with this, Luke Calder! You knew I was expecting to stay at the hotel, and that was the only reason I agreed to come with you. You're nothing but a scheming, conniving, low-down. . .'

'Now, now! Don't you think you're over-reacting? We're both adults, so what harm is there in you staying here with me? Basically it's no different from staying at the hotel.'

'Of course it is! At the hotel there would be other people around, while here. . .' She swallowed hard. 'Here we'll be alone.'

'What a delightfully old-fashioned view! It had never occurred to me that you'd object. Most women I know wouldn't even give it a second thought. Maybe being a Virgo is more than just your star sign and that explains all this maidenly modesty.'

It took a second for what he meant to sink home, then Fran felt colour suffuse her face. 'How dare you? Well, that's it—the final straw. I want you to take me home!'

'Sorry, but I can't do that.' Luke slid the key from the ignition, tossing it lightly in his hand as he opened the car door. 'I'm far too tired to start driving back across town now. Please yourself whether you come inside or not, but you'd be far more comfortable in there than spending the night out here.'

He closed the car door, then strolled towards the house and disappeared inside, leaving Fran staring after him in disbelief. Surely he wasn't going to abandon her out here?

She sat and glared through the windscreen, expecting any minute to see him coming back, but there was no sign of him. Then, as she watched, a light came on in one of the upper rooms, and she shifted uneasily as she recognised Luke as he came to the window and looked out. He couldn't possibly see her in the darkness, but she still shrank down in the seat—then felt her eyes widen when he stripped off his jacket and started to unbutton his shirt.

Fascinated despite herself, Fran could only stare as he pulled the shirt free from his trousers and tossed it aside, then stretched up to open the upper casement, his torso backlighted by the lamp in the room. Even from this distance she could see the way muscles rippled across his chest as he reached up to unlock the window, the wedge of dark hair that arrowed down from his collar-bone, and she felt heat run along her veins. Did he realise that she could see him? Was he doing it deliberately to...to entice her? Well, if he was then he was going to be sadly disappointed!

She turned her gaze away and stared towards the river, watching the faint sway of the trees as their branches dipped and brushed against the water, but after a few too brief seconds she found her eyes drawn helplessly back to that window, and gasped.

The whole house was in darkness, no glimmer of light showing from that window or any other. Far from tempting her by that impromptu strip-tease, Luke Calder had promptly dismissed her from his mind and settled down to sleep!

Taking a slow, deliberate breath to calm the surge of temper, Fran tried to relax, but it was surprising how unsettling the familiar night sounds could be now that she was alone. Why had she never realised before how eerie the rustling of the trees could be, how creepy the sound of the breeze rattling the reeds that lined the riverbank?

Forcing herself to blank the sounds from her head, she stared straight ahead, but found little there to soothe her. *Was* that just a shadow by the house, or was someone hiding there, watching her? She wouldn't put it past Harry Martin to have left someone watching her house, so what if she'd been followed? She was a sitting duck out here all by herself!

With a little moan of fear she scrambled out of the car and raced to the house to hammer on the door, but it opened at the first blow from her fist.

'Changed your mind about coming inside, then?' Luke asked quietly, his face a carefully blank mask, yet she could sense the amusement lurking underneath.

'Yes!' She shot past him into the hall. 'And don't you dare make fun of me!'

'Would I ever?' He closed the door and reached out to switch on the light, making her blink in the sudden flood of brilliant light. 'You didn't need to worry, Fran. I was watching you all the time you were out there, so you were perfectly safe.'

'Watching me? You mean to say that you did that deliberately? You left me out there all by myself, *knowing* that I'd be. . .be. . .?' She couldn't quite bring herself to say the word aloud, but Luke had none of her reservations.

'Terrified?' he laughed softly, leaning easily back against the door as he studied her pale face. 'I just thought that an hour or so on your own would make you come to your senses. Better the devil you know, eh, Fran? And the mind can conjure up no end of devils alone in the night.'

Speechless, she glared at him, then felt the colour start back to her cheeks as she realised for the first time what he was dressed in, which was very little indeed. In a fast sweep her eyes ran from the top of his dark head down to the tips of his elegant feet, and she bit back a groan as she realised that that tempting glimpse of his body had done nothing to prepare her for Luke Calder in the magnificent flesh. Dressed in nothing but a pair of dark boxer shorts that rested low on his lean hips, his body was a tanned perfection of muscles and sinews, living flesh as beautifully sculpted as stone.

She turned away, making a great show of looking round the hallway, afraid that he would read what she was feeling from her expression. 'Well, now that I'm here and you've apparently succeeded in your nasty little ploy, where do I sleep?'

'Follow me and I'll show you which room you can use.' He led the way along the hall and up a winding flight of stairs to the upper level of the house. Fran followed him slowly, keeping her eyes centred on the polished wooden treads and away from the muscled strength of his thighs. When he reached the top of the staircase he turned left along a wide gallery which overlooked the huge living area that encompassed most of the lower level. Stopping at one of the doors, he waited for her to catch up.

'I've put a few things in the room you might need—toiletries and something to wear to sleep in.'

'I'm surprised you have anything to lend me.' She stared pointedly at him, and he laughed softly.

'I don't. I've left you one of my shirts, so I'm afraid you'll have to make do with that tonight. I don't even own a pair of pyjamas—I find them too restricting.'

It wasn't what he said but more the way he said it, imbuing the words with so much meaning that she glared at him. 'I'm sure you do! Well, don't worry, I shall only be here tonight, so I won't restrict your activities for too long!'

She went to move past him into the room, but was forced to stop when he made no attempt to step aside. 'Excuse me, please,' she said politely, but there was nothing polite about the angry, scornful glitter in her grey eyes.

'Are you always this uptight around men, Fran? Can't you ever take a joke?'

'I have no idea what you mean. Now it's very late, and even if you feel like standing there playing games, I don't.'

'Perhaps that's your trouble.'

'What do you mean?'

'That you should learn how to play as well as work.'

'Play? What kind of games did you have in mind? Bedroom ones?' She smiled icily. 'No, thank you. I'm not into playing those sorts of games.'

'With me, or with anyone?'

'That's none of your damned business! Look, I don't know why you imagine you have the right to start probing into my personal life, but take it from me that you haven't. The only dealings we have in common are business ones!'

'So you keep on saying, but I still can't help but remember what it was like out on that deck tonight. Believe me, Fran, I've never concluded a business deal with a kiss like that!'

'Stop it! I won't listen to any more of that nonsense. We've already discussed what happened, and that's it.'

'You think so? Mmm, maybe, maybe not. I know it's going to be interesting to find out. But, as you said, you must be tired. You get on into bed now.' He turned to go back along the gallery, then stopped and looked back at her. 'Oh, and Fran?'

'What?' she snapped, too strung up to even attempt to pretend politeness.

'Sweet dreams.' He laughed softly as he moved away

again, and Fran stormed into the room and slammed the door, but it wasn't that easy to close the door on what he'd said. Until tonight she had never been tempted...by anyone! So what was it about the wretched man that cut straight through her defences? Did he just, from experience, know which button to push, or did this undeniable attraction she felt for him have its roots in something deeper? He'd once mockingly said that their relationship had been written in the stars; if it had been then she was going to have to find some way to unwrite it, fast! Luke Calder wasn't going to get a chance to disrupt all her plans for the future.

She couldn't sleep. Too much had happened today to let her mind rest, although her body ached with fatigue. After tossing restlessly for more than an hour, Fran got up and crept from the room and down the stairs, hoping that a cup of tea would soothe her nerves.

Bypassing the entrance to the huge living-room, which looked dim and shadowy in the faint glow from the circular night-lights sunk into the wooden-slat ceiling, she followed the passageway until she came to another flight of steps, which obviously led down to the lowest level of the house. Cautiously she made her way down them and flicked on the light, gasping in appreciation as she found herself in an ultra-modern kitchen.

The room was done in shades of rich green and stark white, the huge patio doors at the dining end giving access directly on to the garden. With the doors pushed wide open the room and the garden must blend into one, and she was filled with admiration for the skill of the architect who had designed such a harmonious setting.

Still lost in admiration, she filled the kettle, then set about finding what she needed in the numerous cupboards that lined the kitchen walls.

'If you're looking for tea or coffee, try the cupboard to your left, just above the hob.'

She almost shrieked aloud when Luke spoke behind her, whirling round, her face ashen. 'Don't do that! You nearly scared the life out of me!'

'Sorry, I didn't mean to give you a fright. Here, sit down and I'll make that drink.'

He moved further into the room, looking big and commanding against the stark backdrop of the white walls, and Fran felt her mouth go dry. Perhaps it was in deference to her sensibilities that he had slipped on a robe, but it did less to conceal the perfection of his body than to hint tantalisingly at it. Frankly, the last thing she wanted was for him to come too close.

'No! I mean, I can manage if you'll just tell me where everything is.'

He shrugged easily, leaning a shoulder against the wall as he pushed the heavy tousled hair back from his forehead. 'Please yourself. Tea, coffee etcetera in that cupboard. There must be a teapot, but I've not discovered it as yet. Mugs are in the next cupboard along to your right.'

'Fine. I can manage now, thank you.' If she'd hoped he would take the hint and leave her to it, she was sadly disappointed. He stayed right where he was until good manners forced her to offer to make him a drink too. 'Do you want something. . .tea or coffee?'

'Whatever you're having will be fine. I suppose I may as well have a drink now that I'm here.'

'I'm sorry if I woke you up. I tried to be as quiet as possible.' She flicked him a quick glance, then concentrated on lifting two green-patterned mugs from the cupboard and placing them neatly on the marble counter, all too aware that he was watching her every move.

'You didn't wake me. I've been keeping a watch in case we had visitors.'

'Visitors?' That gained her immediate attention and she gave him a shocked look. 'Do you think we were followed here?'

'I've no idea, but it seemed sensible to keep an eye open for anyone in the grounds.' He swore softly when he saw the fear flash in her eyes. 'There's no need to worry—the house is completely secure. In fact, if I hadn't rung through to the police station we'd have had a squad car on our doorstep by now.'

'You mean I've set off the alarms? But how? I saw no sign of them.'

'You aren't meant to. They're highly sophisticated infra-red beams, virtually undetectable to the naked eye. Yet another example of how well designed this whole house is.'

'I see. Then why did you bother losing your sleep if no one can get in? It seems pointless to me.'

'Curiosity.' He smiled almost lazily as he studied her across the brightly lit room. 'You're unwilling to tell me who's at the back of all this, so I thought I'd keep a watch in case anyone turned up and solve the mystery myself.'

His story sounded so genuine that just for a moment

she was tempted to tell him, but something held her back, a deep-seated fear of making a mistake. Until she proved otherwise she had to constantly bear in mind that he might be the enemy. 'There's no mystery. You're looking for answers where there are none, as the police will confirm in the morning.'

He shook his head, his hair catching the light so that it gleamed with a blue fire. 'No, I'm not. You know who's behind it all, Fran—that's why you're so calm. Anyone else would be tearing their hair out trying to work out who was perpetrating such deeds, but you *know* who's doing it!'

'Rubbish! Now if you want that drink you'd better tell me where the fridge is so I can get some milk.' Determinedly she changed the subject, knowing that he was far too astute for her to keep on playing games like that.

'Now that's one mystery I haven't been able to solve. It's there somewhere, behind one of those doors, but I still haven't got the hang of which one it is. Try that one on your left.'

Fran tried the cupboard, but found only dishes, and smiled as she immediately tried the next one along, reaching for the handle at the same moment as Luke came across to help her. Just for a moment their fingers touched, then broke apart as they both stepped back with a haste that would have been comical if it hadn't been for the sudden surge of sensation that arced between them.

'Fran, don't you think. . .?'

She didn't want to hear what he had to say, didn't want to test a resistance that was already weakened.

'You do it.' She laughed shrilly, seeing the way his

eyes had darkened in a way that made the breath lodge hard and heavy in her throat. All at once she became achingly aware of the thinness of the cotton shirt that skimmed down over her thighs, the way the deep V where she had left it unbuttoned at the neck gave glimpses of the top curve of her breasts, and she immediately backed away.

'Stop it!' There was a harshness in his voice, echoed in the depths of his eyes as he glared at her. 'I'm not about to leap on you. What do you take me for, Fran . . .some sort of a monster? I know what kind of an ordeal you've had tonight, and, although I might have been willing to tease you before to take your mind off it and give you something else to think about, I don't intend to ravish you to complete the treatment!'

Tears stung her eyes as she heard his anger and she turned away, rubbing a hand over her eyes to wipe them away, but it seemed impossible to stop the flow now that it had begun. With a little cry of distress she turned to flee from the room, but got no further than a couple of steps when Luke caught her.

'Don't cry. Please, Fran. I didn't mean to upset you, and I can't bear to see you crying.' There was such tenderness in his face as he studied the tears flowing down her cheeks that she cried all the harder. 'Oh, hell and damnation! Come here.'

He pulled her into his arms, giving her no chance to try to evade him as he held her tightly against the solid strength of his body. Fran struggled briefly, but soon gave up the uneven match, letting herself rest against his chest while he stroked her hair with a surprisingly gentle hand. It felt so good to be held close, to feel the warm security of his arms around her. How long had it been since she had let anyone come this close, comfort her, try to ease her fears? It seemed that she had been on her own forever.

Gradually the tears stopped, but still he held her, one hand warm against the ridge of her spine, the other gentle as it stroked the silky length of her hair. Then slowly he set her from him. 'Better now?'

She nodded shakily, feeling cold now that she had lost the warmth of his body. He moved away, walking across the room to stare out through the patio doors, a strange tension in the rigid set of his shoulders. Fran ran a hand over her damp face and smoothed her untidy hair. It had been years since she had cried like that, and that she should have done so now in front of Luke surprised her even more.

She glanced across the room at him, seeing his shadowy reflection in the mirrored glass. Which one was the real Luke Calder: the hard, tough businessman who would stop at nothing and spare no one to get what he wanted, or that tender stranger she'd just had a glimpse of? She wished she knew. A woman should know what sort of a man she was starting to fall in love with.

The thought slid into her mind from nowhere, hitting her such a stunning blow that she gasped. He turned to look at her then, curiosity on his face. 'Are you all right?'

It took everything she possessed to hide the shock she felt. 'Yes, of course. But I think I'll go back to bed now. I won't bother having that drink. I'm sorry for making such a fool of myself just now.'

'You didn't. You just needed to get it all out of your system. It's been quite a night, one way and another.'

There was a strange, reflective note in his voice, but she scarcely heard it, too intent on getting back to her room.

'It certainly has.'

'It doesn't seem that your horoscope was accurate after all, does it?'

'What do you mean?'

'The forecast was that romance would come into your life tonight, but that's hardly been a true assessment of what's happened, has it?'

Why was he watching her like that, studying her so intently? Surely he hadn't somehow read her mind and shared that foolish thought that stress and tiredness had put into her head? That was what had caused it, of course, of that she was convinced, or would be once she'd had time to work on it!

'No,' she snapped, 'it most certainly wasn't. How about yours? Was it any more accurate, or just the load of mumbo-jumbo I said it was?'

Luke laughed deeply, turning away to stare out over the garden again. 'Only time will tell. Ask me again in a couple of months, Fran, and I'll give you the answer then.'

Why did she have the feeling that he knew something she didn't? It disconcerted her. 'I doubt if we'll be in contact in a couple of months' time, so I shall pass on that. Goodnight.'

She hurried from the room, feeling a shivery tingle running down her spine. Something walking across her grave. . .or the forces in heaven laughing at her vain attempts to re-write her future? Whichever, but one thing was crystal-clear and shining brightly through all the confusion: she wasn't going to let herself fall in love with Luke Calder. She wasn't!

CHAPTER SEVEN

FRAN hadn't expected to sleep, but she did, deeply and dreamlessly, and awoke to the sound of birds singing and sunlight streaming in through the window.

The room she was using was at the back of the house, and as she got up and walked over to the window to look out she could see a panorama of fields lying lush and green under a cloudless May sky. Just faintly she could hear the sound of the river, and she opened the window and leant out until she could glimpse it through the trees, the water still shrouded in clouds of early-morning mist. It was an idyllic setting and she would have loved to linger, just drinking in the peace and beauty, but there were too many pressing tasks to be dealt with.

With a regretful sigh she closed the window again and made her way into the luxurious *en suite* bathroom and stripped off the shirt before turning on the shower. It took only minutes under the hot jets to wash the last dreamy remnants of sleep away, and then once again all the previous night's fears came rushing back.

She might be able to convince herself that the momentary flash of madness she'd experienced, in thinking that she was falling in love with Luke Calder, was merely the result of stress, but it didn't change the fact that she was greatly attracted to him, and that was where the true danger lay. She couldn't afford to let her judgement be coloured by personal feelings. If

Luke was involved with Harry Martin in some unsavoury dealings then she couldn't hide the fact. The truth had to be reported, no matter how much it might hurt her to do so.

Fran turned off the shower and wrapped a huge fluffy towel around her to walk back into the bedroom—then came to an abrupt halt when she found Luke standing by the door. Just for a moment their eyes met and locked before she looked away, feeling waves of heat running through her body.

'Did it never occur to you to knock before you came barging in?' she demanded.

'I did knock, several times, but obviously you didn't hear me.' He came further into the room and closed the door, his eyes lingering appreciatively on the soft curves beneath the damp folds of towel. 'I have to admit that I'm rather glad you didn't. Few women manage to look as good as you do in the mornings, Fran!'

If he'd hoped to placate her by the teasing compliment then he achieved the opposite. 'I expect you would be a good judge of that,' she snapped, hating the fact that she felt less annoyed at finding him in the room than at the thought of all the other women he was comparing her to.

He laughed wryly, walking over to the window to stare at the view she had enjoyed such a short time before. 'I've had my share of liaisons, but no more than that, Fran. You flatter me by insisting on seeing me as some sort of Casanova figure. I've always been too busy building up my business to spare time for more than a few brief affairs.'

'People's ideas of what constitutes a "few" differ

greatly!' she shot back, consumed by jealousy at the thought of Luke and other women.

'I expect they do. What would you consider a reasonable figure—one, two, two dozen? Tell me, Fran, how many lovers should a man, or a woman, if you prefer, in these liberated days, have?'

There was an upward quirk to one sleek black brow as he turned round to study her with interest, and she shifted uncomfortably, her bare toes curling into the thick pile of the ivory carpet. 'I have no idea.'

'So you haven't decided on a set number for yourself? You prefer to take a more liberal view and just let things happen naturally without keeping a tally?'

'No! Don't be ridiculous!' She bit her lip, feeling the tension curling in hot little spirals in her stomach as she realised that once again he was slowly and insistently drawing her into one of those disturbingly intimate conversations. 'How many times have I told you that I don't intend to start answering personal questions? Yet you will insist on trying to steer the conversation that way!'

'I do?' He held his hands out, palm upwards. 'I have to plead innocence this time. It was you who started making veiled references to my love-life. I just picked up from there.'

'Well, I want it to stop. . .now.'

'Fine by me. I only came to warn you that I was going out, not to start World War Three. I'll be back in time to take you to the studio, so don't worry about that.'

He started towards the door, stopping with a marked reluctance when Fran exclaimed angrily, 'No! You can't do that. I have to get home. There are things I need to do, quite apart from the fact that the police will be arriving to take fingerprints.'

Luke shook his head, his face set and uncompromising. 'I've already phoned to warn them that you aren't at home. They'll be calling later on in the day.'

'But that's not the point! I can't afford to hang around here waiting until you deign to come back to collect me. Just give me a few minutes while I get dressed and I shall be ready to go with you. You only need to drop me in town, and I can make my own way from there!'

'I'm afraid not—I haven't time to wait. One thing all that experience with women has taught me is how long it takes them to get dressed. I'll see you later.'

'Now just you wait a minute, mister!' She caught his arm, her fingers biting into the soft wool of his suit jacket as she glared up at him with angry eyes. 'Just what gives you the right to try to run my life? You brought me here under false pretences last night, and the very least you can do now is take me back into town! This is just another one of your rotten macho tricks to get me to do what you want, but it won't work!'

'This meeting was set up way before you ever appeared on the scene,' he said harshly. 'It's a working breakfast which I have no intention of cancelling because it doesn't fit in with your selfish plans.'

'Selfish? Me? That's a laugh! When it comes to being selfish then you're top of the league. When have you ever compromised or changed your plans, eh?'

'Many times. Especially since I had the misfortune to come to your aid the other night. I've done nothing but change my plans because of what happened then, and don't you ever forget it.'

'You didn't do it for me! You did it so your precious business wouldn't be harmed in any way!'

'Of course. What other reason would there be?' He smiled suddenly, something in his eyes that made her instantly wary, but when she tried to remove her hand from his arm he covered her fingers with his own and held them there. 'Perhaps I've been a little obtuse, Fran.'

'I don't know what you mean.' She tried to ease her hand out from under his but met with a resistance that could only have been overcome by struggling, and pride refused to let her do that.

'Of course you do. Don't be shy, now. It's a very natural and feminine reaction to resent the fact that I've apparently put business ahead of your wants.'

'Don't be ridiculous! That has nothing whatsoever to do with it. I just don't want to be left here when I have things that need to be done!'

'What sort of things? You can't tidy up the house until after the fingerprint team have been, and I've already told you that I'll arrange for that to be done.'

'I don't want you arranging anything. I can do it by myself, thank you very much!'

'I'm sure you can, but why bother when I can save you the trouble? Has no one ever taught you the gracious art of how to accept help when it's offered?'

'No, they haven't, and I don't intend to learn it either, not when I know there are a whole load of strings probably attached to your generous offer!'

'No strings, Fran, unless, of course, you'd like there to be some.' Luke moved so fast that she had no time to back away as he turned her into his arms and held her to him, so close that she could feel the hard outline of his thighs through the damp towel, the heavy steady beat of his heart against her breast. 'Would it be easier to accept help, Fran, if I set terms of payment? I wonder what the going rate would be?'

His hand slid up her spine, barely brushing against her through the towelling, yet she could feel the heat of it flowing over her skin, and she panicked. 'No! Stop that! What do you think you're doing?'

'Researching the costs, like any good businessman, of course.' His breath clouded on her skin just an instant before his mouth found hers. Fran tried to turn away to avoid the kiss, but Luke slid his hand behind her head and held her firmly as he plundered the ripe, warm swell of her lips. Heat flared along her veins, ripple after ripple of heady sensation that shook her to the very depths. She didn't want to feel this way, didn't want to feel as though her body was burning in the hot fires of hell while her soul was dancing in heaven, but she was powerless to resist the erotic magic of the kiss.

When he raised his head she shuddered, tiny tremors of ecstasy spreading in delicious waves through her whole body, making her limp and pliant in his arms. She stared at him, her eyes cloudy, barely focused, wondering if he felt as stunned as she did.

'Mmm. . .definite possibilities there,' he murmured.

She frowned at him, tossing the hair back from her flushed cheeks, wishing he would take her in his arms and kiss her again instead of making cryptic comments that taxed her stunned powers of comprehension.

He laughed deeply, tracing a finger delicately over the hot swollen curve of her lower lip. 'A possible way of payment. If that's a sample of the kind of terms you're offering, I'm sure we can come to an agreement.'

It was like a douse of cold water, cutting through the lingering remains of passion, and Fran gasped. Wrenching herself out of his arms, she spun away from him, fury written all over her flushed face. 'There will be no agreement, Luke Calder! Never! Once I leave here today that's the last time you and I will meet! You're nothing but a cold, calculating. . .' She floundered for a moment, then rallied again. 'A cold, calculating *Capricorn*!'

He laughed shortly. 'Well, that's true enough, but why object? You were warned what to expect before we met.' He held his hand up, forestalling her angry retort with a cool hauteur that sent her temper flaring. 'Don't bother. We could stand here all day swapping pleasantries, but I don't have the time. I'll see you later. Maybe you'll have cooled down by then.'

He left, and Fran flung herself down on the bed, pummelling the pillow with her fists in a sudden explosion of temper. How did he always manage to turn the tables on her like that? Not once had any man ever made her so mad. . .or roused her to such passion, a tiny treacherous voice whispered inside her head.

She groaned, pressing her hands over her ears, but it wasn't that simple to cut off the insidious little voice. Luke Calder was getting under her skin, and unless she acted quickly she was going to be in serious trouble. She had to make sure that she avoided him in the future and never gave him the chance to pull any more stunts like that! She had her work to concentrate on, and up till now that had been more than enough to fill her life. Let him come back later, but she wouldn't be here: Virgos were quite capable of making plans too!

'By why, Fran? What have you got against the idea? I would have thought that you'd be delighted to invite Calder back just to put your views across again, even though there isn't anything between you both, as you've been at pains to tell me!'

Fran sighed, throwing the pencil down on to the desk as she leant back in the chair. 'I've already explained, Fred. I just don't think the amount of letters we've received justifies giving it more air time.'

'Oh, come on! That's just an excuse. We've had at least two sackfuls in under a week, and we've done follow-ups on the strength of a lot less than that.'

'I know, but I just don't feel that this warrants it!' It had been three days since she'd seen Luke, three days that she'd spent trying to get him out of her system, but she couldn't deny the sudden rush of emotion at the thought of seeing him again. She had half expected him to contact her after she had turned away the team of cleaners he'd sent to her house to clear up the mess, but she had heard nothing. Had he realised that she wanted nothing more to do with him? She hoped so, but she wasn't a hundred per cent certain. Luke Calder wasn't the kind of man to let anyone thwart his plans and get away with it!

Aware that Fred was waiting, hoping to change her mind, she tried again to make him see it her way. 'Let's make a pact, Fred, if we keep on getting mail in any quantity then we shall re-schedule another programme, but if we don't. . .' she shrugged, feigning indifference 'we'll let the whole thing drop.'

'All right. But I still think you're being short-sighted about it.' Fred waved the wad of letters he was holding. 'We thought everyone would be against the development, but opinion seems to be moving the other way, mainly thanks to Calder himself. He made a lot of sense talking about that tip and obviously persuaded people to change their viewpoint.'

'Well, we'll obviously have to bear that in mind, but. . .' She broke off thankfully as the intercom on her desk buzzed. 'Fran Williams.'

'Hi, Fran, it's Judy. There's a meeting on and the chairman has asked me to get you up here to the boardroom.'

'Me? But why?'

'No idea. Shall I tell them you'll be right up?'

'I suppose so.' Fran cut the connection and frowned at Fred. 'Have you any idea what's going on?'

'None at all. I knew there was a meeting on, but your guess is as good as mine why they want to see you.'

'Then I suppose I'll have to go up there and find out.'

She hurried from the office, taking the creaking old lift to the top floor of the building. Judy was at the reception desk and Fran smiled at her before tapping on the door and entering the boardroom. There must have been a dozen people seated round the huge polished table, but she barely noticed any one of them as she opened the door and was confronted by the sight of Luke Calder.

Just for a moment she froze in shock, then became aware of the speculative attention turned her way. Colour swam under her skin, and she moved further into the room and closed the door, feeling as she did so that she was cutting off her last line of retreat.

'Ah, Miss Williams. Please come and sit down.' Hugh Jones, chairman of the board, stood up and waved her to a chair.

Fran sat down, keeping her eyes lowered so that she wouldn't have to meet Luke's eyes across the table, but she could feel him watching her.

'Now I expect you're wondering what this is all about. Nothing nasty, you'll be relieved to know—this isn't the sack, Miss Williams, dear me, no!' Hugh Jones laughed heartily at his little joke, and Fran forced a polite smile from lips that felt strangely stiff. What was going on? And, more importantly, what did Luke Calder have to do with it?

'I expect you've heard the rumours about us seeking further investment for the station—you might even have been privy to some inside information.' Hugh Jones cast her a coy look before glancing meaningfully across at Luke. 'Well, we're delighted to be able to announce that as from today Mr Calder will be joining the board. Naturally he's keen to learn all there is to learn about the business, not just the financial side, but about the programmes we put out, and that's where you come in. It occurred to us that you'd be the ideal person to teach him what goes on behind the scenes.'

'Me?' Her eyes widened in horror. Just for a second her determination not to look at Luke wavered, and she felt her temper rise when she saw the amusement on his face. He was behind all this, wheeling and dealing, playing God! But if he thought he could get away with it he could think again! 'Mr Jones, I'm honoured that you should choose me, but I do feel there are others far more suited to take on the responsibility, people who've worked in radio far longer than I have.'

'Nonsense! You're too modest, Miss Williams. If you didn't have our full confidence then you wouldn't be the front runner on our star programme. You'll be perfect for the job. Now, there are one or two things we still need to discuss, so we'll leave you and Mr Calder to work out some sort of timetable between yourselves.' He stood up, waiting until the others had followed his lead. 'Join us in the dining-room when you've made your arrangements, Luke. We'll drink a toast to your new and undoubtedly fruitful alliance, eh?'

Luke took his outstretched hand, smiling with an easy charm. 'I'll pass this time, if you don't mind, Hugh. I don't believe in wasting time, so if Fran is free for lunch I shall take her out and we can get down to the first lesson.'

'Splendid idea! No time like the present. If more people thought that way the country wouldn't be on its uppers.'

The group left the room, closing the door discreetly behind them, leaving her and Luke alone in the big echoing room. Fran took a slow deep breath and another for good measure, then let rip.

'Don't think you're going to get away with this, you low-down, double-dealing, miserable. . .!'

'Capricorn?' He smiled, mockery dancing in his dark eyes as he studied her furious face. 'Isn't that how the line continues? I seem to remember it rather clearly. You must be upset, Fran, if you're starting to repeat yourself like this.'

'Is it any wonder? What do you hope to gain from

pulling a stunt like this?' She faced him like a small fury, hands on slender hips, breasts heaving with every laboured breath.

'Stunt? I've just made a huge investment in this station and you call it a stunt?'

'And what else would you like to call it?'

'A sound business venture. I've looked into the potential of the station and am satisfied that it's a good investment. This isn't a stunt. I intend to make a great deal of money from this if my speculations are correct.'

'Then why do you need to involve me?' She smiled sweetly. 'You've obviously done your homework and are satisfied, so what's the point of this charade? You're no more interested in how a programme is put together than you are in flying to the moon!'

'Oh, but I am. I might have checked out the financial aspects of buying into the station, but one thing I've learned over the years is that you can never do too much research. Surely you must remember how thorough I am, Fran?'

His voice was deep and soft with memories, so that she felt her heart dip, then beat crazily as she remembered the last time she'd been involved in his research, when he'd kissed her that morning. She shook her head, trying to clear the hot rush of blood that made her feel strangely dizzy. 'I *remember* telling you that I wanted nothing more to do with you!' she snapped.

'On a personal level, yes. But this is business.' Luke moved round the table and came closer, so that she had to tilt her head to look up into his face, and that— and only that!—increased the whirling inside her head.

'Whatever business we had together is concluded,' she said quickly. 'It was over the night I accompanied you to that dinner and backed up your story. There hasn't been a word in the papers nor any hint of a rumour around town, so that's it as far as I'm concerned. I've kept my side of the bargain and I expect you to keep yours.'

'Of course. But is it my fault if my business dealings somehow keep on involving you?' He smiled slowly down at her, his gaze centring on her mouth in a way that made it start to throb. 'We seem destined to keep crossing paths, as though our lives are linked in some mysterious plan.'

'I... Nonsense!' Fran tried to inject a dash of disdain into the denial, but it was hard when he kept looking at her mouth that way. For three whole days she'd blanked out the memory of that kiss they'd shared, but now it came flooding back with a vengeance, hot and strong and so seductively real that she could have wept for shame. Luke Calder was nothing but a ruthless manipulator who made people do what he wanted when he wanted it, yet all she could think of was that she *wanted* to feel again the hot urgency of his mouth!

'Probably.' He quirked a dark brow when she failed to respond. 'I no more believe in destiny than you apparently do. I, too, deal in facts, Fran, and the fact is that, like it or not, we have business together again.'

'And at whose instigation? You expect me to believe that the board just chose me at random? Huh!'

Luke shook his head. 'I doubt if it was at random. It's common knowledge that you were at that dinner with me. I expect they just put two and two together and went on from there.'

'But you had nothing to do with their choice? You

never asked for me?' Why did it hurt to learn that it had been the machinations of others that had brought them together this time? She didn't know, and lost no time dwelling on it.

'Not specifically, no.'

'I see.'

'So does that mean you'll teach me all you can about your job?'

'I'm hardly in a position to refuse, am I?' She started to leave, then stopped when he called her back.

'Haven't you forgotten something, Fran? We have a lunch date.'

She knew she would regret it later, but the urge to get one up on him just once was far too strong to resist. 'Sorry, but I make it a rule never to have working lunches—so bad for the digestion, I find. However, I shall be available in my office from about one-thirty onwards if you have any questions you'd like to ask me. Perhaps I'll see you then.'

'Oh, you'll see me, all right. I'm looking forward to working with you again. You must admit that last time was an. . .an interesting experience.'

There were so many double meanings in his voice that Fran felt a tremor race hot and cold to the tips of her toes. Just for a second longer she hovered uncertainly in the doorway, fighting against the urge to beg him to find someone else to teach him before she spun round and ran from the room. He'd called their previous alliance interesting, but she would not have called it that. Devastating was the word that sprang to mind, so devastating that she wasn't sure she could handle a second shot!

* * *

It had been a mistake. It would have been better to accept the lunch date after all. At least there would have been some measure of impersonality about a restaurant, whereas here, trapped in the confines of her small office with Luke so close, there was a definite air of intimacy.

'So you work several weeks in advance, then?' he queried.

'What?' Fran blushed crimson as she realised that he was staring at her, one corner of his mouth lifted mockingly as though he could read her thoughts.

'Scheduling,' he repeated blandly with a patience that didn't fool her for an instant. He knew how uncomfortable she felt and he was enjoying every single minute of it!

Hurriedly she forced herself to pay attention, surreptitiously edging away from him so that her arm no longer brushed against his every time he moved. That was part of the trouble, of course: she was just so aware of him. The office had never felt this small and cramped before, not even when the whole team held a meeting there. Yet half an hour of Luke's presence in the room and she was becoming claustrophobic.

'We try to plan well in advance, but obviously we have to be flexible. There are times when items of special interest must take precedence over any schedule. The success of the *Day-to-Day* programme lies in the fact that we try to stay on top of the news.'

'I see. It must be quite a task, even in a small town like this.'

'Oh, we don't confine ourselves to the town. We cover the whole of the surrounding area to give a wider view and report on events that might at some time affect the town.'

'And who does all the research?' Luke leant forward, narrowing the space once again, so that, despite herself, Fran felt her pulse leap in a heady response.

Immediately she moved away again, perching precariously on the very edge of her chair, and heard him laugh softly.

'Sorry, Fran. Was I invading your space again? I always forget how uptight you are about that.'

'I have no idea what you mean. Now, shall we confine ourselves to business? That's why you're here, after all, isn't it?'

'Of course,' he agreed smoothly, leaning back in the chair to stretch his arms above his head as though sitting still had cramped his muscles. His jacket fell open, revealing the strong contours of his chest under the thin white cotton of his shirt, and Fran found her eyes drawn to the faint shadow of body hair she could see beneath the thin fabric. Abruptly she looked away, hating him, hating herself, hating everyone for putting her in this horribly vulnerable position. She didn't want to feel this attraction for Luke Calder and would fight it every inch of the way.

'The whole team works on each programme at different stages, starting with one of the researchers, who makes all the preliminary enquiries. Once that's done and we're satisfied that our guest has the ability to talk on the air then it goes ahead.'

'And how do you check that the guest will be able to talk once he or she is on the show? How do you know that you haven't landed yourself with someone who'll be struck dumb with nerves?'

She shrugged. 'There's no guarantee, but you can soon assess a person's ability to talk sensibly. Usually we ring them up, have a short conversation with them over the phone and then take it from there.'

'The way you did with me? You telephoned me at the hotel and had that long conversation with me.' He laughed cynically. 'There was I, feeling flattered at the attention you were paying me, when all the time you were just testing me out to see that I wouldn't dry up on the air! Do you give scores for those pre-interview performances, Fran? I'd love to know what mine was.'

'No, we don't. We just try to make certain that a guest will be comfortable with a certain line of questioning.'

'Comfortable?' He shot her an amused glance. 'I didn't notice you trying to make me "comfortable" during that interview. I had the distinct impression that you were out for the kill!'

'Sometimes interviews can move in a different direction from the one you anticipate,' she said shortly, knowing that there was more than a grain of truth in what he'd said.

'And that's why you go to such lengths to ensure you research your subject even down to the fact of their star sign?'

'No! I explained that to you. That was just Debbie's little aberration. I've given her strict instructions never to do anything like that again!'

'It bothered you that much, did it?'

'It didn't *bother* me at all. Stop trying to put words into my mouth. I just didn't feel that it was justified, adding notes like that to the file when she could barely uncover all the relevant facts.'

'And that's all you're ever interested in, facts, not feelings or hunches?' he asked quietly.

'Of course. If more people confined themselves to dealing with facts then life would be a whole lot simpler.'

'I agree, yet somehow I find it difficult to accept that you live entirely by that principle.' Luke settled back in the chair, crossing his long legs as he stared sideways at her. 'The fact was that you needed help to sort out your house the other day, yet you turned away the team of cleaners I hired, and why? Because your emotions got the better of you. Isn't that right?'

'That has nothing whatsoever to do with any of this!' Fran jumped to her feet and swept a hand angrily around the office. 'This is supposed to be a business arrangement, not some opportunity for you to start delving into what makes me tick!'

'Of course. Sit down, Fran. We still have a lot to cover yet. We can't afford to waste any time on tantrums.'

'I am not having a tantrum!' She sucked in a huge breath, then let it out slowly again. 'Listen, I don't know what you're up to now, but let me make it quite clear that I'm only prepared to put up with you for the sake of the station and my job. This is business—pure and simple.'

'I'm in complete agreement. For the next couple of weeks while I get to know how the station works I shall be like your shadow, Fran, but you'll have the comfort of knowing that it's all in the line of business.'

'Couple of weeks? But I thought a couple of days . . .less.' There was no disguising her shock, but Luke just smiled at her, his face betraying nothing.

'I wouldn't insult you by thinking I could learn enough in a couple of days. Oh, I know what you're going to say,' he put in, forestalling her attempt to speak. 'That I must be far too busy to spare that much time out of my schedule, but don't worry about that. Everything is flowing remarkably smoothly at present, so I can afford to give you my undivided attention for the next couple of weeks. Yes, wherever you go, Fran, I go too. . .and all strictly in the line of business, of course.'

What could she say? What could she do? Nothing! He had out-planned her, outmanoeuvred her and backed her into the proverbial corner! How was she going to survive two weeks of his company when a mere two days would disrupt her whole life?

CHAPTER EIGHT

FRAN'S nerves were raw, so strung up that she could feel her hands shaking as she fastened her bag and picked up her tape-recorder from the desk. She walked to the door, trying her hardest to ignore the man who fell into step beside her.

For a couple of days now Luke had trailed her round the station, sat in her office, watched her through the glass partition of the control-room as she'd done her interviews: everywhere she had turned, he'd been there, and she couldn't take much more.

Wrenching the swing door open, she strode out of the building and headed for the street. Her car was still in the garage waiting for a visit from the insurance assessor before work could start on it, but she didn't need it to get into town. She would walk the half-mile or so, and if Luke didn't like the idea then he knew exactly what he could do about it.

'Where are you going? My car's in the car park. Come on.' Luke tried to steer her across the road, but she turned on him, her eyes heavy with shadows, her face pale and strained. She'd had difficulty in sleeping these past few nights, although she was exhausted from trying to clean up the house after she finished work each day. She was just too keyed up with everything that had happened—the break-in and Luke's unwelcome and disturbing presence in her life—to rest. Now all the strain caught up with her and she snapped.

'I don't want you to drive me anywhere. I'm walking into town, and if you don't like the idea then hard luck. You know what you can do about it!'

She walked on, her body trembling despite the warmth of the sun. May had burst into full glorious bloom, turning the surrounding countryside into a scene from a painting with its rich greens and golds, but Fran could draw no pleasure from it. Her whole life seemed to be dominated by just one man, so that she could concentrate on little else.

'You need a rest, Fran. I've been watching you these past few days, and you're incredibly tense. It's no wonder, of course, when you think of what's happened to you, but if you don't watch it you're going to crack. Haven't you any holidays coming up?' Luke strode along beside her, hands pushed easily into the pockets of the leather jacket he was wearing over jeans and a blue knit shirt that made his skin look even more tanned, his hair richly black. Everything about him assailed her senses in a way she resented bitterly yet seemed unable to do anything about.

When she didn't answer he sighed roughly, increasing his pace so that he could walk in front of her and force her to stop.

'Do you mind?' she bit out waspishly. 'This might be just a game to you, but I'm working, and I'm going to be late if you hold me up!'

'There's over an hour before the meeting is due to start. You won't be late even if you insist on walking into town rather than accept a lift off me. You aren't going anywhere until you tell me what's wrong.'

His arrogance goaded her beyond bearing. 'And who

do you think you are, to tell me what I can and can't do? Don't overstep the mark too far, Mr Calder!'

'I happen to be a major shareholder in the station now, so that makes me your boss if you want it spelling out to you. And the name is Luke. Don't try distancing yourself from me by calling me Mr Calder. Frankly, after what we've been through together that's nothing short of childish. We both know what's eating you, and it won't be solved by juvenile behaviour!'

'Then what will solve it? Come on, *Luke*, you're the boss, the one with all the answers, so explain how I can rid myself of this resentment I feel at having you foist yourself on me again!'

There was an edge to her voice that bordered on hysteria, and his eyes narrowed. He glanced round, then caught her arm and steered her unceremoniously across the street into a small park, holding her so tightly that she had no chance to break away.

'Stop it! Let me go, you big bully!' Despite the fact that she knew that it was pointless, Fran began to struggle, pride and a fierce determination not to give in making her twist and turn in his hold. He stopped abruptly, glaring down at her from eyes that looked like dark chasms.

'You just won't try and make it easy for yourself, will you? You're so damned stubborn!' His anger matched her own, then outgrew it so that she felt her breath catch in dismay as she saw the expression on his coldly furious face.

'Luke, I. . .' She got no further, the words swallowed up as he bent and took her mouth in a punishing kiss that stole her breath from the very first touch of his lips. There was no warmth in the kiss, no hint of that wild hot passion she remembered so vividly, just a cold, ruthless determination to make her bend to his will. When he let her go she stared up at him with anguish in her eyes and heard him swear roughly, viciously.

He swung away from her, walking over to the edge of the small pond, his body rigid with a tension that made her afraid to do or say anything that might unleash that anger once again. She half turned to go, then stopped, unable to understand the strange reluctance she felt at leaving him with this bitter anger lying between them.

She walked over to the pond and bent to pick up a small pebble, skimming it across the glittering water, watching the way it bounced, then sank, leaving behind it only ripples.

'Why do you keep fighting me, Fran?'

Luke's voice was so low that she had to strain to hear it above the noisy chatter of the birds, the rustle of the breeze in the trees. She glanced down, dusting the dirt from the pebble off her hands, wondering how to answer such an unanswerable question. What would he say if she told him that she fought him because she was afraid that if she didn't she would fall in love with him? She had no idea, but there was no way she would tell him that anyway.

'I wasn't aware that I was fighting you,' she said at last.

'Oh, come on! Don't lie, to me or yourself. You know damned well that if I said black was black you'd say it was white!' He thrust his hair back from his forehead with a lean, impatient hand. 'Ever since we met you've been acting quite out of character.'

'And who says it's out of character? What makes you think you know anything about me and the way I act?'

'Because I've spent the last day or so watching you with other people, and frankly, Fran, it's obvious to anyone that when you're with me you act far differently.'

'Maybe I just don't like *you*! It might come as a huge blow to your ego, but there are women in this world who won't fall in a gibbering little heap at your feet every time you spare them a smile or a word. I'm just one of them.'

'Ah, so that's it: you don't like me?' His mouth curled into a slow smile that sent unease rippling through her just as swiftly as that sinking pebble had sent ripples chasing across the pond.

'No! We're just not. . .compatible!'

'So that explains why you're always so tense when I'm around and why we always seem to end up bickering?'

'Probably. We just don't hit it off, that's all.' It was hard to conceal the sudden rush of nerves she felt when she saw the way he was watching her with that barely hidden amusement.

'I see. Well, it's good to have some sort of an explanation I can give everyone. There have been a few comments passed about the way you're behaving, but don't worry, next time I hear anyone discussing it I'll set them straight.'

'Do that, and, while you're about it, try to remember that we're colleagues, and that *colleagues* do not go around kissing one another! If you feel the need to vent your ill temper then choose another way!'

'Of course. You have my word, Fran, that I'll never kiss you again. . .in anger. Fair enough?'

It wasn't fair, not a bit, the way he could side-step and outmanoeuvre her with such ease. Now she would spend the next week or so wondering when and *how* he was going to kiss her!

'Thank you, Councillor. I appreciate the time you've given to answer the questions.' Fran switched off the tape-recorder then glanced across the crowded foyer, immediately pin-pointing Luke in a group clustered around the door to the Council Chamber. He had kept out of her way while she'd been interviewing but she had been aware of where he was all the time. He was seemingly engrossed in conversation, although she couldn't see with whom because of the milling crowd round the doorway. Then, as she watched, the crowd parted and a man came towards her.

Fran turned away, trying to hide her shock at seeing Harry Martin here. He passed her by without a glance, but she could feel the cold waves of antipathy issuing from him, and shivered. She turned to watch him leave, experiencing a second shock as she recognised the man who was driving the car that arrived to collect him as one of the pair who had waylaid her in the car park.

'How's it going? Fran?'

She jumped when Luke spoke her name, spinning round to face him. Just for a second she met his curious gaze then looked away, feeling her heart pounding in a way that made her feel sick.

It appeared that she'd been right about Harry Martin's being behind the attempts to intimidate her.

Had she been right about Luke's involvement with him too? They had both apparently been part of the group clustered around the door; had that been mere coincidence, or had it been Harry Martin that Luke had been so engrossed in talking to? Suddenly the need to know the truth once and for all was too great.

'I've just about finished here. It went better than I hoped, probably because everyone is anxious about giving the right impression, with the May elections coming up.' Fran forced herself to sound cool and friendly, to betray no hint of the fear twisting her heart at the thought of what she might discover. 'We may as well call it a day now, though. Tell you what, I'll buy you a cup of coffee to make up for my bad temper before.'

Luke stared levelly at her, his eyes betraying nothing as they centred on her face. 'That's a sudden change of heart! I thought the last thing you wanted was to have to spend more time than necessary in my company. . . seeing as you dislike me so much?'

Colour flared in her cheeks, but she met his gaze with equanimity. 'I was rude before and I apologise for it. I've not been sleeping well since the house was ransacked, and it's made me very edgy. You. . .well, you just seemed to catch the rough edge of it.'

'I can understand that all right. I was surprised to learn that you were staying there again by yourself.' He stopped, studying her consideringly for a moment. 'I take it that you do live there by yourself, Fran? It's something I've never actually asked you about.'

'Of course I do!' She gave a rather shrill little laugh, feeling the intent scrutiny like a physical touch. 'Who else do you think is there with me?'

He shrugged, taking the recorder from her to loop the strap over his shoulder. 'Who knows? Mother, father, sister, brother, husband, lover? We haven't spent much time discussing our personal lives, have we?'

'No.' She drew in a short quick breath, hating what she was going to do yet knowing that it was unavoidable in her quest for the truth. 'Why don't we make up for lost time, then, Luke? We can have a coffee, talk, maybe get to know one another a bit better. After all, we're going to have to work together for the next week or so, so maybe it will help iron out the problems we keep having.'

'Maybe, but I'm afraid I shall have to pass on that offer of coffee. There are a few things that have cropped up which I have to see to now. Let's make it dinner tonight instead.'

'Well, I. . .' Fran hesitated, something about the glint in his dark eyes making her wary of accepting.

'You did say that you wanted to patch up our differences, Fran?'

'Yes, of course I do.'

'Then dinner would be the ideal opportunity.' He smiled easily, taking her arm to steer her towards the door. 'I'll walk you back and collect my car, then pick you up around seven. That'll give us plenty of time to talk.'

Why did she have the sudden feeling that she was no longer in control? 'Well, I don't know.'

'Surely you haven't changed your mind already?' He stopped on the top step to look down at her, and there was no mistaking the mocking glitter in his eyes now.

'I never took you for a person who constantly changes her mind, Fran.'

'No! I mean, no, I haven't changed my mind. Dinner will be fine. Have you anywhere particular in mind?'

'Oh, I'm sure I can think of somewhere suitable, somewhere nice and quiet where we won't be disturbed while we have our little talk. Leave it to me, Fran, and trust me to make all the arrangements.'

Trust him? She'd as soon trust a rattlesnake when he looked at her that way! Why, oh, why had she ever started this? Because she had to know once and for all what was going on, that was why.

The sun was sliding from the sky, streaking the clouds with vermilion as it went. Fran picked up her bag and went downstairs, remembering the last time she'd got ready to go out with Luke. A lot had happened that night, more than she cared to dwell on now, but one thing she had to remember was her vulnerability to him. She had agreed to this dinner to try to find out the truth, and she mustn't allow the attraction she felt for him to cloud that.

The bell rang as she reached the bottom of the stairs, and she hurried to answer the door, feeling her pulse skip a beat when she found Luke standing on the step. Dressed in a charcoal-grey suit and white shirt, he looked more handsome than any man had a right to look, and she felt her resolve slip for a moment. How could she get through an evening in his company when everything that was female in her responded to him in a way that knocked her totally off balance? If she did discover that he was involved in some shady dealing, then could she honestly trust herself to stick to her principles?

'Ready?' He quirked a dark brow, his eyes lingering with open appreciation on her slim figure in the silky pale green dress, and Fran felt the first whisper of heat run along her veins.

'I'll just get my coat,' she said hoarsely. She swung round and hurried along the hall to get her coat from the closet, willing the sudden rush of attraction to abate, then jumped when he spoke from just behind her.

'I see you've managed to get most of your things back into place, Fran. What have the police said about the break-in? Have you heard anything from them yet?'

She shook her head, lifting her coat down from the peg, her heart beating double time as he came and took it from her to slide it smoothly up her arms. 'Nothing as yet. They didn't find any fingerprints, so I doubt if they'll come up with anything.'

He smoothed the creamy wool across her shoulders, his hands lingering as he turned her firmly to face him. 'Why don't you tell them what you know, Fran? What are you hiding? Has it something to do with the story you're working on?'

'Why do you think that?' Her voice was sharp with suspicion, and his eyes narrowed thoughtfully.

'Because that's the only explanation that makes any kind of sense. I'm right, aren't I? You're on to something, and all this is the result of it. But can't you see how foolish you are to try to handle this by yourself?' Luke shook her slightly, his hands tightening almost painfully on her shoulders. 'No story is worth risking your life for!'

'It isn't a question of risking my life!'

'Isn't it?' His eyes seemed to mesmerise her, draining her will, forcing his own upon her. 'Tell me what's going on, Fran. Make me understand why you're willing to take such a risk for the sake of a story.'

'No, you have it all wrong.'

'I haven't. Don't try to lie to me! Tell me, let me help you, dammit, before it's too late!'

Help her, or help himself by warning his friend how much she knew? The cold worm of suspicion crawled on and she pulled away. 'You're being melodramatic, Luke. There's nothing to tell you about. Stop letting your imagination run away with you.'

He smiled thinly with little amusement. 'You forget, Fran, that, as a Capricorn, everything I do is based on hard fact, not imagination. I prefer to think things through and find a logical reason for them, and reason tells me that you're hiding what information you have from the police because you're afraid that it will ruin your scoop. But one thing you should understand is that you're in way over your head. Unless you help yourself soon then you're in real danger.'

'Is that a threat?' She instantly regretted the question when she saw the expression that crossed his face.

'Why should I want to threaten you, Fran? It isn't the first time you've implied that I know something about what's going on, so how about explaining it to me?'

'There's nothing to explain.' She forced the quivery feeling of revulsion down, realising that she was arousing his suspicions. 'I'm sorry. I explained before how on edge I am at the moment. I'm not accusing you of anything, Luke. Just forget what I said. . .please. If you want to call this dinner off then I understand.'

He seemed to weigh up her words, then smiled thoughtfully. 'No, I don't want to do that. I think the best thing we can do is leave any talk of work until tomorrow and concentrate on the real reason why we agreed to this evening and get to know one another better.'

'That seems sensible to me.' She picked up her bag and led the way along the hall and out of the front door. 'Where did you decide on in the end? It was rather late notice to book a table.'

'Mmm, that's what I thought, so I decided to take you back to the house to eat.' He urged her forward, his hand firm under her elbow as he steered her down the path towards his car. Fran dug in her heels, glaring angrily up at him when he was forced to stop.

'You said that we'd be going to a restaurant!'

'Did I? I don't remember. I *do* remember saying that we'd go somewhere quiet so we can talk without any interruptions, and what better place to choose than the house?' He looked calmly back at her, the breeze ruffling his hair across his forehead. 'It isn't the first time you've been there, so I didn't imagine that there'd be a problem about going there tonight.'

No, it wasn't the first time, but remembering what had happened previously, how he had kissed her and, worst of all, how she had responded, she knew it was the last place she would have chosen when she needed to keep a clear head! Yet if she voiced her objections it would only serve to alert him to how uneasy she felt.

'There isn't a problem. I'm just surprised that you've bothered going to so much trouble, cooking a meal.'

Luke took her arm again, opening the car door to help her inside. 'It was no trouble. There's a housekeeper employed to attend to all that. MacAllister offered me her services when he let the house to me.'

He closed the car door and slid behind the wheel, shooting Fran a level look. 'I don't want to press-gang you into doing something you're not happy with, so if you have any reservations just say so. I can always ring the house and let her know there's been a change of plan.'

Fran shook her head, easier now that she knew they wouldn't be there alone. 'No, there's no need. As you say, it will be peaceful there, so we can talk.'

The engine roared smoothly to life and he pulled away from the kerb. 'That's one of the joys of living there—the peace and quiet.'

'It must be. How long have you rented it for?' She snatched at the chance to make small talk while she got her emotions strictly under control again.

'I'm not too certain. It was all done in a rush. I got the offer of the house, but I've no idea when MacAllister will be back.' He turned down a side-street, slowing as he slid in behind another vehicle. 'He's the architect in charge of the development, you know?'

'Is he? Well, he seems very talented. That house is a joy, the way it harmonises with the countryside.'

'That's one of the reasons why I'm so confident about what we're planning on building. James MacAllister's number-one priority is always that any building should be in keeping with its setting.'

'I see. If he does as good a job on the new houses

then no one will object.' She drew in a silent little breath, feeling her heartbeat running into triple time with nerves. 'I take it that everything's sorted out and ready to go ahead, then? Is there any local investment in the project, or does it just involve you and the builders?'

'We've had offers locally, but nothing has been agreed as yet.' Was it her imagination, or was there a faint hardening to his voice? She didn't want to make him suspicious, but she had to know.

'So everything is on course, then?'

'Apart from a slight hiccup over a tract of land, yes. Why?' Luke turned to study her, his eyes narrowing slightly. 'You seem very interested all of a sudden, Fran. Why is that?'

She shrugged, glancing away from the searching gaze to stare through the windscreen. 'Just curiosity, that's all. After all, I live here, so it's only natural that I should be interested in what goes on.'

'And that's the only reason?' He slowed the car at a junction, letting the engine idle, his face set. 'Why do I have the feeling that there's more to it than that?'

'I have no idea. Imagination, I expect.'

He laughed softly. 'I've already told you that I'm not prone to letting my imagination run away with me. It isn't in my nature. Maybe I do fit the bill of the perfect Capricorn after all.'

'Maybe you do.' Fran smiled dismissively, feigning uninterest in the subject, although her heart was beating rapidly. She would have to go carefully, ask her questions in a way that wouldn't make him suspicious, maybe change the subject for now. 'You said that you left the town when you were a child, yet you appear to know your way around. Is it just from memory?'

He slid the car into gear and edged out on to the main road, waiting until he had overtaken a pair of cyclists before replying. 'Partly from memory, I expect. The town has changed surprisingly little over the years. Oh, there's been some development on the outskirts, but the centre hasn't altered all that much.'

'Why did you leave here? Did your parents have to move because of their work?'

'My mother wasn't married. I never knew my father, or indeed who he was. She always refused to tell me.' He smiled grimly, letting the car's speed increase so that the hedges whizzed past in a green blur. 'Thirty years ago having a child outside marriage wasn't considered to be the accepted thing. My mother had a tough time trying to make ends meet. That was the reason why she fell in with the man she later married. I think she was grateful to him for bothering to show any interest in a woman with an illegitimate child on her hands. He took us back to Scotland with him.'

His voice was hard with memories, and Fran shivered. 'Didn't you like him. . .the man she married?'

'Like?' He laughed, a bitter sound that made her ache for all the pain it conveyed. 'I don't think it's possible to like a sadist, do you? He beat my mother black and blue, and then when she was too worn out to fight back he turned his attention to me. . .until I grew big enough to beat him back!'

'Oh, that's awful!' Unconsciously she reached out and laid her hand on his arm, wanting in some way to offer comfort for a pain that was still hurting despite the passage of time. 'You must have hated him for what he did.'

'At the time I did, but later I came to appreciate it. I was always a sensitive child, but he beat it out of me, taught me that the only way to make your way in life is by standing up and fighting for what you want. I guess I owe everything I've achieved so far to him!'

Luke turned the car off the main road, taking the back lanes leading to the river. 'Enough of my life story. What about you, Fran? What made you the woman you are today?'

She shrugged, still hurting at all he'd suffered, although she knew instinctively that he wouldn't thank her for it. Just for a moment she let her hand linger on his sleeve, then slowly withdrew it, wondering if she was glad or sorry that he had given her such an insight into what made him the man he was today. With such experiences of life it would be no wonder if he had few scruples about how he got what he wanted. Life had given him very little, just taught him to snatch any opportunities that came his way and use them to his advantage. 'I had a far happier childhood than you did, from the sound of it. Very normal—father, mother, and me as the adored only child. It was an idyllic upbringing, until. . .' She stopped abruptly, suddenly wondering what she was doing, telling him about her life.

Luke drew the car to a halt in front of the house and cut the engine, turning in the seat to face her, his eyes so black that she could see tiny images of herself reflected in their depths.

'Until what, Fran?' he prompted gently. His voice seemed to draw her to him, making her want to tell him things that she'd told no one. 'Tell me, Fran. It's obviously something important, something that still hurts you—and, believe me, I can understand that.' He took her hand, linking his long, hard fingers between hers, joining them in a physical as well as a mental bond, and suddenly Fran knew that she wanted to tell him the one thing that had fashioned her into the woman she was. Maybe if he understood that then he would understand why the truth was so important to her.

'My father was a schoolteacher, a very gentle man.' She laughed sadly. 'Ever read Chaucer, the description of the knight in *The Canterbury Tales*? My father was like that, the "parfit gentle knight", who would hurt no one, believed in honour, truth, courtesy, all those old-fashioned virtues that no one has any time for. When he was accused, quite erroneously, of siphoning money from school funds he honestly believed that everyone would realise that there'd been a mistake.'

'And did they?' His fingers tightened slightly on hers, bringing her eyes up to meet his steady gaze.

'No. Oh, perhaps they would have done, if it hadn't been for the local newspaper. They went to town on the story, piled up what they saw as the evidence against my father until everyone, it seemed, thought he was guilty.' Tears clouded her eyes as she remembered those dark days, but she blinked them away. 'The strain of it all brought on a heart attack. My father died, and two months later so did my mother. And do you know what was the worst thing of all—do you?'

Luke shook his head. 'No. What?'

'A few weeks later it was discovered that the money

had been stolen by one of the members of the Parent Teacher Association. Oh, the local paper printed an apology—I made sure of that! But by then it was too late to rectify the damage they'd done.'

'And that's when you decided that the truth should always be reported, no matter what?'

'Yes!' She stared back at him, cold fear numbing her heart. 'And that's why I'll never compromise, Luke. . . never!'

'Why do I get the idea that that's a warning?' He laughed shortly, little amusement on his face. 'What are you really up to tonight, Fran? What games are you playing?'

She drew in a shuddery breath, praying she hadn't gone too far and alerted him. 'No games. You invited me to dinner and I accepted; that's all there is to it.'

He shook his head, his eyes dark as glass as they studied her. 'There's a lot more to it than that. But for now I'll go along with you. Let's go inside and have that dinner I promised you.'

He got out of the car, waiting for her to join him. Fran walked with him to the door, wishing that she had never agreed to this in the first place. She wanted to turn tail and run and keep on running away from him, away from what she might discover, away from what could only break her heart, yet she knew that was impossible. Their two lives were already linked, one interwoven with the other. How could she change what seemed to be written in the stars?

CHAPTER NINE

THE air was heavy with the scent of flowers. Fran picked up her glass and took a sip of the wine before resting her head back against the cushion. She had imagined how the room would look with the patio doors pushed wide open, and the reality hadn't been a disappointment. They had eaten the delicious meal to the sound of the river flowing past while the sun faded behind the skyline. Now it was soothing to just sit out on the terrace and watch the night unfold.

'You're very quiet. Are you tired?'

Luke's voice was soft, in keeping with the peace of the night, and she responded just as softly, not wanting to disturb the magic of the moment. 'A bit, but pleasantly so. It was a lovely meal, Luke, made all the more so for being eaten in such a setting. Aren't you tempted to try and buy this house for yourself?'

'Very, but I doubt if MacAllister would sell it. He designed and built it specially for his wife because she'd always wanted to live by the river, but she only had time to enjoy it for a few months before she died. It obviously means a lot to him.'

'How sad.' She was surprised to feel tears mist her eyes and brushed them quickly away, hoping that he wouldn't notice. 'He must have loved her a lot.'

'He must have done.' He moved closer, reaching out to turn her face towards him so that the light glittered on the tell-tale mist on her cheeks. 'What's the matter? Have I said something to upset you?'

There was such masculine bewilderment in his deep voice at the unexpected display of emotion that Fran smiled.

'Not really. It was just me being silly. It seemed so sad that Mrs MacAllister should have had so little time to enjoy this beauty and that he should be left here by himself.'

'It's not silly at all.' He brushed his thumb across her cheek, wiping the wetness from her skin but leaving behind the sensation of fire on her flesh. 'This is what makes you so special, Fran, this ability to feel for others.'

'Special?' She gave a light, forced little laugh, moving away from the touch of his hand, which was wreaking such havoc on emotions she had tried so hard to keep under control. 'I doubt that I'm special just because I get upset when I hear something sad. Most women feel the same.'

He shook his head, settling back again in his chair, his eyes fixing on the silvery ribbon of water swirling away between the trees. 'No, they don't. In my experience most women take what they want from life without a thought for whom it hurts. They wouldn't recognise emotion if it stood up and hit them!'

'That's a dreadful thing to say! I don't know what kind of women you've associated with, Luke Calder, but, believe me, it must have been the wrong kind!'

He smiled wryly. 'Probably. Oh, I'm not complaining—I've always made it my business to ensure that the women I meet are the sort who understand the rules and know how to play the game. I never wanted to get involved with any of them emotionally. I just needed them for a purpose, and that was enough.'

She flushed when she grasped his meaning, hating the cold cynicism in his voice. 'That's a horrible thing to admit!'

'I expect it is, but it's the truth, and you're the last person to condemn me for telling the truth, even though it may offend you to hear it.' He turned to face her then, his eyes intent as they met hers for one long minute, and she had the strangest feeling that he was trying to look inside her soul. 'Why did you come here tonight, Fran?'

It was hard to think while he was watching her like that, and even harder to follow the sudden switch in the conversation. 'I. . .you know why. We decided to try to get to know one another better, seeing as we're forced to work together for the next week or so.'

'And that was the only reason?'

'Of course! What are you implying, Luke?'

'Just that sometimes the truth is far harder to admit to than lies.'

'I don't know what you mean.' She set the glass down on the table, her hand shaking so that it rattled against the ornate white-painted metal. Suddenly all the magic had gone from the night and all her previous fears returned. She had wanted so desperately to find out the truth about Luke, but now that was the last thing she wanted to know.

'I think you do, Fran. I think there's a lot that you aren't telling me.' He didn't move, yet she could sense the tension in him, feel the burning power of his gaze. 'You came here tonight for several reasons, but none of them was to smooth our working relationship, so why lie? What are you trying to hide?'

'Nothing!' Fran came to her feet in a rush, heart pounding, colour fading from her skin. 'I think it would be better if I left now—this conversation is in danger of deteriorating into yet another verbal battle. Thank you for the dinner, but I'm afraid it's all been a waste of time. There's no way that we can ever hope to get along better than we already do!'

'No.' Luke was on his feet and in front of her before she could take a step towards the doors. 'You're not running off yet, Fran. Not until you give me a few answers and do me the courtesy of telling the truth.'

'You can't stop me leaving!' She bit her lip to stem the rising panic, her eyes huge and frightened, and heard him curse.

'I'm not going to hurt you! All I want is a few answers, then you're free to leave any time you like.'

'I want to leave now! You want answers? To what? What are you trying to bully me into saying, Luke?'

'I'm not bullying you into anything. Don't be so dramatic. All I want is the truth, the real reason why you decided to come here, why you suggested that we try to ease our differences in the first place.'

'Then I'm afraid you're going to be sadly disappointed. I don't have any answers. I obviously made a huge mistake in thinking that we could *ever* learn to tolerate one another. Now please get out of my way.' She tossed her head, sending the silky swath of hair tumbling over her shoulders, and sensed rather than saw the sudden shift of emotion away from anger to a raw wild passion that stole her breath and made her legs go weak.

'And if I refuse? What will you do then, Fran? How will you make me get out of your way when you know deep down that that's the last thing you really want me to do?'

His voice was warm velvet, soft, smooth, sliding over her to send her senses reeling, and she had to fight to hang on to her control. Anger she could handle, as she could handle the cold knives of fear, but this soft, warm seduction was something beyond her.

She licked her parched lips, feeling her breath coming in laboured little spurts as the blood eddied along her veins, consuming her with a heady passion. 'I. . . I'll shout for help.'

Luke laughed deeply, his eyes glittering with tiny flames of excitement. 'But who will hear you? We're a long way from anywhere here, Fran. That's part of the charm of this house.'

She looked round almost wildly, her hands clenching and unclenching as tension pulled every nerve tight. 'The housekeeper. . .?'

'She left half an hour ago. Didn't you realise?' He moved closer, until just a few inches separated them, staring down into her eyes with intent written all over his face.

'No!' She backed away, one hand raised to ward him off, stopping abruptly as she came up against the edge of the table. 'You can't frighten me, Luke Calder,' she said hoarsely. 'You can't scare me into telling you what you want to hear!'

'Who said anything about wanting to frighten you?' He moved again towards her, trapping her between the table and the hard, dangerous warmth of his body. 'That's the last thing I have in mind.'

He reached out and let his hand trail up her bare arm, watching her face as his fingers slid over the smooth silk of her skin. Fran closed her eyes, willing the frantic pounding of her pulse to slow, but when his fingers completed their slow journey and came to rest at the base of her neck she knew that he could feel every frantic beat.

'Feel it, Fran. Feel how you respond to me? That's one truth you can't lie about.' His voice was pure seduction, drawing her deeper and deeper into the spell of passion, and she shook her head with a desperation born of fear—fear not of him but of what she would do if he continued this heady, drugging assault on her senses. 'No, you're wrong!'

'I am? Maybe we should test that out.' His hand curled around the back of her neck, slipping under the heavy weight of her hair, and she shuddered violently, her whole body so tense that she felt she would shatter into a thousand tiny pieces.

'Please, Luke,' she whispered brokenly, opening her eyes to stare at him.

'Please. . .what?' He drew her closer, easing her slight weight against the hard warmth of his body. 'Please kiss you? That's one request I'm only too willing to grant.'

He bent to take her mouth, but with the very last vestige of control she turned her face away so that his lips skimmed hard and firm along the line of her jaw.

'No! You mustn't. This is madness, Luke. You don't know what you're doing!'

'Oh, but I do. I know exactly what I'm doing, and why.' He caught her chin to turn her face round so that he could look straight into her eyes. 'This is something

I should have done days ago; something I've wanted to do almost from the first moment we met, yet I've fought against it every step of the way, just as you have. But why fight it now? Why try to rewrite what's already mapped out for us?'

He held her gaze as he lowered his head and took her mouth in a kiss that was little more than a whisper of sensation, a fleeting brush of one soul against another, and Fran shuddered. If he had kissed her with passion or some brutal demand to impose his will on her then she could have found the strength to fight him, but there was no way she could resist this aching tenderness, this joining that made them one whole.

Beneath her curled fist she could feel his heart pounding, feel the heavy rhythm of his life ticking away in so many years, so many days, so many hours. Who knew what life held in store for either one of them? All there was as a certainty was here and now. This moment would never come again. She had to snatch it now or lose it forever. Who cared if it was right or wrong, who cared if it was truth or lies? She loved him, and that was all that mattered.

Her hands slid up his chest, her fingers uncurling against the hard wall of muscle, tracing every strong lean line until they brushed against the warm skin of his throat, then slid on to draw his head back down while she kissed him just as tenderly, just as achingly as he had kissed her.

'Fran?' Her name was a prayer, an ache of need, a question, and she reacted instinctively. Taking his hand, she led him back inside.

They made love slowly at first, taking their time smoothing away clothing to dress each other's bodies in kisses, to learn the new yet strangely familiar contours. Why did it feel so right to have Luke stroke his hand along the curve of her thigh, to feel it slide up over her hip and dip into the hollow of her waist before moving on to the fullness of her breast? Why did she feel no embarrassment or fear at letting her fingers trace down the hair-roughened muscles of his chest to skim the flat planes of his stomach and then move on? This was the first time they had shared such intimacies, yet there was a familiarity about the touch of muscle and skin, the shape of flesh and bone. Her body knew his touch, just as she knew how to touch him to make his heart beat, feel his pulse quicken.

There was no explanation and none she needed as passion rose, carrying them to heights Fran had never imagined. But as Luke joined with her and experienced the first brief resistance of her untutored flesh she felt the shock run through him. He went rigid, his head lifting as he stared into her eyes for one brief moment that held all eternity within it.

'Little Virgo!' he bit out, but there was more triumph in the exclamation than accusation. Fran laughed softly, meeting his gaze as she twisted her hips up to his.

'Not any longer!'

Then everything was movement, sensation, and she could no longer laugh or speak or do anything but be carried along by a force greater than anything she had ever known before, a force that took them to the heavens to touch the stars that had already decided their destiny.

* * *

It was raining, thin trickles of water sliding down the window, tainting the air with dampness.

Fran watched the raindrops running down the glass panes, wishing foolishly that the sun had been shining again as a sort of omen. Beside her, Luke stirred briefly, his hand curving round her waist to draw her closer, and unconsciously she stiffened.

He seemed to sense her withdrawal somehow, because his eyes opened slowly, focusing immediately on her face.

'Don't, Fran.'

She tried to turn her head away, but he turned it back with a gentleness that was deceptive.

'No, I won't let you feel guilty. We did nothing wrong. We made love, that's all.'

All. . .it was everything! She drew away from him, shivering as she left the warm circle cast by his body, and heard him sigh as he raised himself up to stare down at her.

'Nothing will change what happened, Fran—you know that. Don't make it hard on yourself.' He smoothed the tangled hair back from her face, letting his fingers linger against her skin. 'Don't spoil something beautiful when there's no need.'

'Was it beautiful, Luke? It wasn't just my imagination? You felt it too?' There was a need for reassurance in the whispered question, and he smiled gently, rolling her over to gather her close in his arms.

'You know it was—more beautiful than anything I've ever experienced in this whole world.' He pressed a kiss to her lips, his mouth warm and sweet and tender, and she responded eagerly, wanting the reassurance only he could give her. Somewhere between the time when they had fallen into an exhausted sleep and when she had woken to this grey dawn, all the joy and magic of what they had shared had faded, and she had been overcome by doubts. Now, as his mouth covered hers and his hands slid down to cup her breasts and tease the nipples into eager life, she felt again the power and the passion that made everything right.

She loved him, so much that it seemed impossible that she had lived her life this long without him, impossible that he couldn't know it from her response. Surely he must feel something for her, otherwise they could never create such magic?

This time there was no gentleness in his lovemaking, no slow, sensual forays. His hands moved over her with knowledge now, stroking, caressing, bringing her within minutes to the point where she was clinging to him, wanting only the satisfaction he could give her. She reached up, holding his face between her hands, drawing his mouth back to hers to kiss him with an open-mouthed urgency that sent them both spinning out of control.

When at last they lay quietly, her head resting on Luke's shoulder, her hand spread against the damp warmth of his skin, Fran felt as though she had come back from some great journey that had shifted her conception and understanding of everything. This was all that was important now, this love she felt for him and one day hoped he would feel for her.

'Are you all right?' His voice was rough, his breathing still laboured, and she smiled, enjoying in a very feminine way what she could do to him.

'I'm fine. More than fine. Fantastic!'

He laughed at that, pulling her closer to skim a

shower of kisses across her cheek before nibbling seductively at the lobe of her ear. Fran shuddered, feeling the reawakening passion curling in waves through her, one after the other. She turned to him, pressing her mouth to his in a long, drugging kiss, while her hands slid tantalisingly over his hips in a blatant invitation.

Luke groaned, dropping back against the pillows and closing his eyes. 'Witch! Have you no shame, tempting an exhausted man like that?'

'Should I have?' Her hands moved on, stroking him, enjoying the differing textures, smooth and rough, silk and velvet. He caught her exploring fingers and lifted them to his mouth and kissed them quickly, his eyes filled with a wry mockery as he studied her flushed face.

'Much as I'd like to go for a hat trick, my sweet, I have to admit that I'm not Superman. The spirit is more than willing, but the flesh is decidedly weak.'

'Oh!' Fran flushed even more, trying to draw away, but he wouldn't let her as he curled her to him and held her tightly until the ache subsided.

'Better?' His voice was filled with tenderness, his eyes dark with understanding, and she nodded, loving him more than ever at that moment.

'Yes,' she whispered, stroking a finger delicately along his jaw, needing somehow to touch him even if it was only now so innocently. 'I'm sorry, Luke. It's just that I. . .'

She stopped abruptly, suddenly afraid to say the words aloud in case they were words he wouldn't want to hear. One night and morning didn't give her the right to confess her love when it might just be a burden to him.

'Just that...what?' He looked curiously at her, watching the shadow darken her eyes to a stormy grey. 'What is it, Fran? What were you going to say before you thought better of it?'

She shrugged, feeling her skin sliding against his as she moved. 'Nothing. It doesn't matter.' She kissed him hard and quickly, then spun out of his arms, dragging the cover off the bed to wrap around her.

'Mmm, that seems rather pointless to me. I know every square inch of your delectable flesh, Miss Williams, so well that I could paint every luscious curve from memory.'

She glared at him in mock severity, glad that he had let the question drop. 'Don't even think about it! Just humour me, eh? This is all new to me.'

'So I realised.' He slid up against the pillows, looking so devastatingly sexy with his rumpled hair and heavy eyes that Fran felt her heart jolt to a stop. 'That's something we have to talk about, Fran. It shocked the life out of me when I realised you were a virgin. You should have told me.'

'How?' She smiled as she turned away from the tempting sight of him, holding the swaths of cotton around her as she crossed the room and picked up his hairbrush to untangle the knots from her hair. 'It isn't the sort of thing one announces, is it? You know, "Hello, I'm Fran Williams and I'm a virgin".'

He laughed. 'I guess not. But why, Fran?'

'Why what?' She dropped the brush, winnowing the pale strands of her hair with her fingers to loosen the stubborn tangles.

'Why choose to give something so precious to me?'

There was no laughter now, no mockery, and she went still, wondering how to answer the question, how to explain that the reason was that she loved him.

'Well?'

She shrugged, avoiding looking at him. 'I don't know. Maybe it just seemed the right time, and the right place. . .'

'And the right guy?' Luke shook his head, his eyes filled with certainty. 'I don't believe that. There was more to it than that.'

'Well, if you discover what then please tell me.' She stood up, anxious to stop the conversation heading into uncharted territory. 'While you're thinking about it I'll go and take a shower.'

'Be my guest. But don't think I'm going to let it drop. I'll find out your reasons, Fran. . .one way or another.' There was a taunting sexual threat in the words, and she smiled at him over her shoulder as she paused in the bathroom doorway and let the cotton coverlet slide from her shoulders to land in a heap at her feet. 'I can hardly wait!'

She spun into the bathroom and locked the door, smiling to herself as she heard him leap from the bed, too late to catch her. This whole thing was a new experience to her. She had never indulged in this sort of banter, never tasted the heady joys of teasing until the teasing had to stop when passion broke through to the surface.

She switched on the shower and tested the water, then looked round for some shampoo to wash the rest of the snarls from her hair. There were dozens of bottles ranged along the smoked-glass shelves, but not one of them contained shampoo. Leaving the shower running, she unlocked the door, but there was no sign of Luke in the bedroom.

Lifting the white towelling robe from its hook behind the door, she slipped it on and hurried from the room and along the balcony to find him, smiling when she heard the low rumble of his deep voice coming from downstairs in the living-room. She ran down the stairs, then paused in the doorway, not wanting to break in on his telephone conversation.

'No, she's been here all night. You don't need to worry. I'll try to keep her here as long as I can if it will help.'

Fran frowned, staring at the broad expanse of his bare back that was presented to her. He was obviously talking about her, but to whom, and why?

Curiosity rather than a desire to eavesdrop kept her hovering in the doorway, and she felt her blood start to run cold at what she heard.

'No, I've already told you. I still don't know what she's uncovered. She hasn't said anything about what she's working on, but give me time. She'll tell me, all right, and then we can go from there and decide what to do for the best. All I want right now is to make sure that she doesn't cause any more trouble. It's vital that she doesn't do that! I. . .'

Fran must have made some noise, some movement, some tiny betraying gesture, because he swung round, his face hardening when he saw her in the doorway. Abruptly he terminated the conversation and put the phone down, not moving his eyes from her face. Fran took a slow deep breath, then another and another, but there was no way she could hold back the knifing pain.

It had all been a trick, all that sweet, hot loving, that tenderness, just a cruel device to help him find out what she knew.

'Well done, Luke! I have to give you top marks for determination. This should put you right at the top of the list of Martin's favourite people.' Her voice was like thin sharp ice, but not cold enough to fully hide the pain, and she hated herself for letting him hear it.

'I have no idea what you're talking about. Martin who?' His accent was more pronounced now, grating in a way she had never noticed before. Was he worried that she'd finally found her proof that he was hand in glove with Harry Martin? She hoped so!

'Why pretend? We both know what's been going on. How long have you and Harry Martin been working together? Is it a recent alliance, or does it stretch back a few years and involve a few other deals? Come on, Luke, you can't leave me with only part of a story. That's just being a spoil-sport.'

'You've been looking into Harry Martin's activities?' He phrased it as a question, but she didn't bother dignifying it with an answer, and he continued in the same grating tone. 'So he's the one behind everything that's been happening to you recently.'

'And of course you didn't know a thing about it, did you?' She laughed bitterly. 'Really, I think I knew you were in on it all along. Everything that happened was just too pat, too convenient. You rescued me from those gorillas at the garage, took me out to that dinner and, lo and behold, I came home to find my house ransacked by someone who must have known how long

I'd be away. And of course there was last night!' She moved suddenly, unable to stay still as she walked into the room and stared at him with contempt. 'That was the real triumph, wasn't it—getting me here, persuading me to stay the night? It's just a pity that all that effort you expended was wasted really. I'd never have told you what I know, no matter how many times you made love to me!'

'No?' He had her by the arms before she could move, his face like granite as he glared down at her. 'Don't you believe it, sweetheart. I had you eating out of my hand last night! A couple more nights and you'd have told me anything.'

Shame rose in a hot wave, governing her actions, defying caution. Her hand came up and she caught him a stinging blow across the cheek, watching without a flicker as the mark turned first white, then red.

'Why, you little. . .' He gripped her so hard that her bones grated together, and she gasped in pain before stumbling as he pushed her away. He walked away, his whole body rigid with tension, his hands clenched into fists, his face like a mask. 'Does that make you feel better, sweetheart? Restore your precious virtue in some strange way?' He shook his head, contempt flowing into his face. 'You accuse me of underhand dealing, of using dubious methods to get what I want? I have to hand it to you, Fran, you have a lot of nerve!'

'I don't know what you're talking about!' she snapped. Now that the rush of anger had abated just as quickly as it had risen she felt cold, icy tremors rippling along her veins.

'Come on. Why pretend? You made the supreme

sacrifice of your life for your work last night, so don't be shy about admitting it. There can't be many women who'd go to such lengths just to get a story! Most expect a lot more than that when they sell their bodies.'

'Sell their. . .' Colour rose in her face and she stared at him in horror. 'You can't really believe I went to bed with you just for a story?'

Luke shrugged lightly, almost dismissively, as though the subject was starting to lose interest for him. 'What other reason? I must admit to a certain degree of hurt masculine pride that it wasn't me who tempted you, but, as a businessman and a major shareholder in the station, I have to admire your dedication. With employees like you I'm almost guaranteed to turn over a profit for my investment.'

How could he even think that, let alone say it? Hadn't it meant anything to him? Hadn't he understood that she had given herself to him for the only reason that made any sense to her. Even the pain of finally finding out that he and Harry Martin were painted with the same filthy brush didn't hurt as much as that careless indictment. All that was left to her now was pride—pride not to let him know how much he had hurt her, pride not to let him find out how much she loved him.

'Sometimes one has to make sacrifices to achieve an objective.' She smiled, her jaw aching from the effort of holding back the tears. 'I intended to find out about your involvement with that man, and now I have, although I must admit I'm still a little bit hazy as to the details. I don't suppose you'd care to go into a few details. . .a little extra payment for last night?'

Luke's face darkened like thunder, his eyes murderous as he stared back at her. 'You've had all you're going to get from me, lady! Now I suggest that you get your things together. I want you out of here within ten minutes.'

'Of course. I never did intend to outstay my welcome.' She turned to leave, wondering if her legs would hold her when she felt like crumpling in a heap at his feet.

'Oh, and Fran, another suggestion for you.'

She paused in the doorway, holding on to the wall as she felt the weakness spreading. 'What is it?'

'Only that you don't rush into making too much of what you've learned this morning. I doubt if you've any hard facts to go on yet, so don't make the mistake of being too hasty. You could come to regret it.'

'Suggestion. . .or threats? Careful, Luke, your true colours are beginning to show. Don't worry about me—I know exactly what I'm doing. Just warn your friend Martin to be extra careful, because everything he does is under close scrutiny. However, just to set your mind at rest, seeing as you're so concerned about my welfare, I shall make a point of telling the rest of the *Day-to-Day* team what's been going on. If anything happens to me then you can rest assured that they'll carry on with it. Look on it as an extra bit of security for all that money you've invested in the station. It seems you can't actually lose either way, doesn't it? The good old Capricorn business acumen coming up trumps again!'

Fran walked away, holding on to her control with a bitter determination. She wouldn't cry. She wouldn't break down. She wouldn't let him see that he had hurt

DESTINED TO LOVE 161

her in a way that Harry Martin and all his tricks could never have hurt her.

She would never let him know that he had broken her heart.

CHAPTER TEN

'AND you're sure you're feeling better, Fran? You don't look so good, if you want my honest opinion. Still rather pale. You haven't come back to work too soon, have you?'

'No, I feel fine, Fred. . .honestly.' Fran smiled, her face aching from the effort it cost to make the lie seem like the truth. She had phoned in sick straight after she'd got home that dreadful morning and spent the next couple of days trying to come to terms with what had happened, but there was no way she could ever accept what Luke had done, how he had used her in that unscrupulous way. Somehow she had to learn to live with the pain of the deception and get on with her life, but she knew it was going to be the hardest thing she had ever had to do.

'Well, if you're sure. I must say, I'm glad you're back. We've been inundated with calls from listeners wanting to know where you were. Nice to know that you're missed, eh, love?'

'It is.' Her smile was more genuine now, less strained. 'I did wonder if you'd find someone to replace me and I'd be out of a job.'

'No way! You've made this programme yours, Fran, and the public wouldn't be happy to accept a substitute. I was only saying as much to Calder when he called yesterday.'

'He. . .he's still around, then, is he?' It was hard to

stop the sudden rush of emotion just the mention of his name could provoke, but she did her best. Luke Calder's presence at the station was a fact of life, and she had to learn how to handle it or give up her job, and pride would never allow her to do that and let him know he had won.

'Funnily enough, no, he isn't. We haven't seen hide nor hair of him while you've been off. But he phoned yesterday and seemed a bit put out when I told him you were ill.'

'I'm sure he did. Probably wondering if it would have some sort of adverse effect on his investment!' There was a cutting note in her voice, and she coloured when she saw Fred look at her.

'Do I get the idea that all isn't going well between you two?' he asked quietly.

She shrugged. 'You could say that. Look, Fred, there's something I think you should know, just in case—well, in case something happens to me.'

'Happens to you? What's this all about, Fran?'

'Just that I've found out a bit more about our friend Martin's business dealings, and, more importantly, who he's dealing with. Oh, I've had my suspicions for a while now, not that I was the only one. Even Terry Lewis hinted at it when I spoke to him the other evening. However, now I can state quite categorically that. . .' She broke off as the office door opened and Debbie burst into the room. 'Yes, Debbie?'

There was a curtness to her tone, but Debbie didn't seem at all perturbed as she grinned at them both. 'I thought you'd want to see the paper, Miss Williams. I managed to get a copy of it before it hits the shops. I know you've been investigating that horrible Martin man, even though you've tried to keep it quiet, so here you are.'

She thrust the paper across the desk, then was gone almost as fast as she'd come. Fran stared at the headlines, feeling sickness welling into her stomach. Quickly she read the article, then handed the paper to Fred, wondering why she felt as though the bottom had just fallen out of her world. It didn't bother her one bit that Terry Lewis had claimed the scoop by reporting that Harry Martin, along with two local councillors, had been charged by the police with fraudulent land dealing. What did bother her was the realisation that very soon Luke could find himself part of the same mess.

Why should she be worried about him, after what he had done? He didn't deserve it, yet she couldn't stop the cold sick waves of fear she felt at what might happen to him. Suddenly she knew that she had to warn him. She might despise him for the methods he used in business, but the fact remained that she loved him, and if there was anything she could do to protect him she would do it.

She jumped to her feet, her face white, her eyes haunted, her heart beating painfully at the thought of what she had to do. 'Will you lend me your car, Fred? I wouldn't ask, but it's important.'

He only hesitated for a moment before something about the strained tension on her face made his mind up. 'Of course. Here are the keys. It's over the road as usual.'

'Thanks, Fred. I owe you one for this.'

He shook his head. 'Just be careful, and make sure

you know what you're doing—that it's the right thing, whatever it is.'

Fran smiled shakily, picking up her bag from the desk. 'The whole trouble is that I'm not sure what's right and wrong any more, Fred. All I know is that I'll regret it all my life if I don't do this now.'

She ran from the office and hurried from the building and across the road to the car park. Fred's car was old and difficult to start, but at last she managed it, and headed out into the street. She had no way of knowing where Luke was this morning, but it seemed logical to try the house first and then go on from there.

He wasn't at the house, but the housekeeper was. Fran exchanged pleasantries with her, curbing her impatience before finally asking if she knew where Luke had gone, and went weak with relief when the other woman informed her that he had gone to the old college.

Refusing the invitation to go in for coffee, Fran hurried back to the car and drove across town, only slowing when she turned in through the gates of the college and made her way along the rutted gravel path to pull up in front of the old sandstone building next to Luke's car. She cut the engine, then sat with her hands clenched round the steering-wheel, suddenly uncertain what she would say to him. She must have been mad to come like this. What would he think? What would——?

Every coherent thought fled abruptly as a tall figure appeared round the side of the building. He stared at the unfamiliar car for a moment, then his face hardened as he recognised her. Fran took a deep breath then opened the door, willing her legs to support her as she walked across the weed-strewn gravel towards him.

'Hello, Luke.'

He didn't bother to answer, just dipped his head in the barest acknowledgement, his face like granite, his eyes devoid of expression. Fran felt her heart turn over, her stomach knot, but she forced herself to stand there under the cold stare.

'I had to see you,' she told him.

'Why? I thought we'd seen enough of each other to last a lifetime. I can't see that there's any need to waste more time.' Luke turned to walk away, but she caught his sleeve and stopped him.

'Wait! You don't understand.'

'What don't I understand?' He smiled thinly, looking pointedly at her hand, and she let it drop to her side. 'Don't tell me you've suddenly discovered that you might have made a mistake about me? Hard luck, sweetheart, but I don't want to hear, if that's what this is all about. Now, I'm a very busy man, and I really don't have time to stand here listening to you any longer.'

'Don't you?' The pain was intense, gripping her with its cruel talons, biting deep, but not so deep that it wiped out the sudden rush of anger she felt at his blind stubbornness. 'Well, I suggest that you make time! I didn't come here to apologise. I came to warn you!'

'About what? That you're going to do a story about my involvement with Martin?' He laughed bitterly. 'Forget it, Fran. You try making anything out of that and you'll find yourself up to your neck in more trouble than you can handle!'

'I'm not trying to do any story—I don't need to now.

Terry Lewis has already got there ahead of me.' She tossed her head defiantly, and just for a moment saw a flicker of something in his eyes before it was gone so fast that she knew she must have imagined it. 'I didn't come here to argue with you, Luke. I came to tell you that Harry Martin has been arrested for fraudulent land dealing. It's all over the front pages of the local paper.'

'And you imagine that I'll be the next to be arrested? What did you expect to gain from coming here, Fran—that I might suddenly decide to make a full confession?' He shook his head, his eyes filled with contempt. 'Sorry, but you're in for a disappointment. I have nothing to confess.'

'I didn't come for a confession! I came to warn you what had happened in case there was anything you. . . anything you can do to help yourself. Look, I don't know a lot about this sort of thing, but surely it would go in your favour if you went to the police and told them everything of your own accord without waiting for them to. . .to. . .?' Fran broke off, staring at him with frightened eyes.

'Arrest me?' he said softly. 'I don't think there's much danger of that.'

'Why? Because you imagine that Martin will do the gentlemanly thing and keep you out of it? Like hell he will! He'll drop you in it as fast as he can if it will help him, Luke!'

'I'm sure he would if he could. I've dealt with many men like him over the years and I'm under no illusions as to his character. I wouldn't be where I am today if I couldn't hold my own in a dog-eat-dog world. I'm not worried for one reason and one alone, the best reason in the world. Don't you know what it is even now?'

'No, I don't. Stop playing games, Luke—there isn't time for that. It might only be hours before the police start questioning you!'

'So what are you suggesting: that I make up some nice little story? That I tell lies, Fran, to save my neck? That doesn't sound like the sort of advice I'd expect to hear coming from you, with all your high ideals!'

Her face flamed and she glared at him, wondering if there wasn't a grain of truth in what he said. Why had she come here to warn him if she didn't expect him to lie? 'No, that wasn't why I came.'

'Then why did you come?' His voice softened, the deep tones strangely vibrant with an emotion she found impossible to recognise but which sent a little quiver of warmth through the cold ice in her veins.

'I've already explained. It would be better if you contacted the police rather than wait until they arrive to question you.'

'I'm sure it would, if I had anything to tell them, but I don't, Fran.' He reached out and caught her chin, tilting her face so that he could look deep into her eyes. 'Listen to what I'm telling you, Fran. . .really listen. Then maybe you'll understand why I'm not at all worried.' He let her go, smiling faintly at her.

'You're saying that you aren't involved with Harry Martin?' There was disbelief in her voice, and the smile faded, leaving his face once again cold and remote.

'I'm saying nothing at all. I've said everything I intend to say. Now it's up to you to work out the answers all by yourself.'

'But that morning at the house, when you were on

the phone. . .' She tailed off, colour coming and going as she remembered what had happened both before and after that fateful conversation she'd overheard, and saw in his eyes an echo of everything that she was feeling. Suddenly everything shifted slightly out of focus, all the certainty that she was right about his being involved, and she was left feeling totally disorientated. Had she added up the facts wrongly, found him guilty more because it was what she had feared than that it was the truth?

'Having doubts, are you, Fran? Wondering if you jumped rather hastily to conclusions?' There was a cool sarcasm in his tone that stung, and her head lifted.

'Maybe. So why don't you put an end to it here and now and tell me the truth? Or are you too afraid to actually admit that the great Luke Calder could ever stoop to underhand dealing to get what he wants?'

'The truth is staring you in the face, but you're too blind to see it. Obviously you need time to think everything through. Call me when you get it all straight in your head, my sweet.' He strode past her, crossing the gravel in a few long strides to open the door of his car.

'Where are you going?' she demanded. 'Are you going to act on what I told you, or what?'

'If by that you mean am I going to the police station to confess, then no. I have work to do, the same as you have. But don't worry, I have no intention of trying to skip the country! If the police need to talk to me then they know where I'm staying, the same as you do.'

'I won't be contacting you again! I don't want anything more to do with you, Luke Calder!'

'No?' He leant his arm along the top of the car door,

letting his eyes rest on her face for one moment that felt like half a lifetime to her. 'It's not that simple, Fran. Oh, you'll try not to let it happen, but tonight, when you're lying awake in your bed, unable to sleep, you'll find yourself wondering again and again about what's happened. You're already experiencing some doubts about it, aren't you? But by tonight those doubts will become almost more than you can stand.' He smiled suddenly, his face softening for a moment. 'It's harder than anyone imagines to outrun destiny, I think.'

He got into the car and started the engine to drive back down the path. Fran stared after him with tears in her eyes and an ache in her heart. She wanted to scream and shout, to deny what he had said, but she knew it was no use. Luke Calder was her destiny.

Had it been a prophecy, or had Luke merely implanted the idea in her head? As she climbed out of bed and opened the curtain Fran had no idea which it was, but he'd been right. It was barely five a.m. and dawn was just breaking, but she was wide awake, as she had been all night long. She had spent those long sleepless hours going back and forth over everything that had happened, every word they'd spoken, everything she'd seen, and at some point had come to realise that she'd been wrong. She had no evidence to back it up, but in her heart she *knew* that Luke would never deal with a man like Martin, no matter how much he stood to gain from it.

She turned away from the window, sighing wearily as she glanced round the room. It was one thing to realise the mistake she'd made and quite another to rectify it. She had accused Luke of acting in the most despicable way possible, so what hope was there that he would ever accept her apologies? She had ruined their relationship, and she would live with the pain of that for the rest of her life.

The telephone suddenly rang and she started nervously before hurrying to answer it. 'Yes?'

'So I was right, then. You are awake?'

Just the sound of Luke's deep voice was enough to bring tears to her eyes, and she swallowed hard before whispering brokenly, 'Yes.'

'So now that you've had time to think things through, what conclusion have you come to?'

'I. . .' It was hard to put into words what had been until so recently just a thought at the back of her mind, but she had to try. However, he seemed impatient to hear what she had to say.

'Come on, Fran, don't keep me in suspense! Don't you think you owe me this much at least?'

He was right, of course; she did owe him the courtesy of an apology, even though he would very likely throw it back in her face. 'I was wrong, Luke. I've spent the night thinking about everything that happened, and I now realise that I made a mistake about you being involved with Harry Martin.'

There was silence for a moment, a silence so deep and intense that she could hear her own heart beating, almost hear the flow of blood rushing through her veins. Then he spoke, his voice not quite as calm as it had been previously, the accent humming roughly in the depths of the tones.

'Are you sure about that, Fran? You have no proof

one way or the other, so can you really believe it without that?'

'Yes.'

'Why? How can you now suddenly decide that this is the truth when you were so convinced before that I was guilty of every form of unscrupulous dealing possible?'

It was little wonder that he sounded loath to believe her change of heart at this stage, and she wanted desperately to convince him, but how? How could she admit that she had reached her conclusion not by logic or reasoning but by sheer gut feeling brought about by the love she felt for him?

'I. . . I just thought it all through and realised I was wrong. I can't explain it any better than that, Luke!'

There was a touch of desperation in her reply which she knew he heard, but surprisingly he made no attempt to mock her, or force her into giving him any more reasons. When he spoke again his voice was warm and deep, and so tender that all the tears spilled over and slid down her cheeks.

'You don't need to explain any more, Fran. I understand. I think I've known how you feel for some time now. Don't cry, sweet. It'll be all right.'

'How do you know I'm crying?' She sniffed back the tears, wiping her face on the sleeve of her nightgown.

'Because I can feel your pain, Fran. But save your tears. There's no need for them now.'

'Luke, I. . . Luke! Luke!' She stared at the silent phone for a second, then slowly replaced the receiver and clasped her hands uncertainly in front of her. Why had he hung up like that? Had he accepted her apology? If so, then what would happen now, or was that just the end of it?

There were no answers, or none that she could find, short of calling him back and asking, and she wouldn't do that. If this was the end then she needed time to come to terms with it by herself. She wouldn't embarrass either of them by making a scene.

She showered and dressed, then caught the early bus into town and walked the rest of the way to the radio station. The building was deserted at this hour of the morning, the corridors echoing as she made her way to her office and sat down behind the desk. But by the time the rest of the staff arrived she had done no work, had just sat staring blankly into space.

'My, my, you are the early bird, Fran. Couldn't you sleep?'

Fred breezed into the office, his lined face breaking into a disbelieving grin when he found her already behind the desk. Fran gave him a watery smile, then turned her attention pointedly back to the schedule to forestall any further questions, and Fred took the hint. They worked on the following week's agenda until mid-morning, only breaking when Fred was called away.

Fran ran a hand wearily over her face, closing her eyes, feeling the tiredness from the sleepless night catching up with her. She leant her head back against the hard cushion on the swivel chair, not bothering to open her eyes when the door opened again.

'Got everything sorted out, then, Fred? I hope so. I don't feel much like juggling with the scheduling this morning.'

'You should try getting more sleep.'

Her eyes flew open and she stared in shock at Luke, who was standing by the desk. Just for a moment her eyes lingered hungrily on his face before she looked away, terrified of what he would read on her own face. 'I didn't expect to see you here.'

'No? I am a major shareholder, if you remember. And after this morning I'll be even more than that. Hugh Jones has decided to step down from the chairman's seat and the board has asked me if I'd be willing to take over from him.' He came closer to the desk, sitting easily on one corner of it so that their eyes were almost on a level. 'We'll be working even closer together from now on, I expect.'

'I. . .' Fran felt as though someone had just knocked the breath out of her and fought to speak. 'Congratulations, Luke. You must be pleased by their confidence in you.'

He shrugged easily, his shoulders moving under the formal dark suit he was wearing to such devastating effect. Whatever he wore he looked marvellous in, and Fran's heart tripped alarmingly as she appreciated how attractive he was for the umpteenth time.

'I am. I think I can help the station with its planned expansion, and even add a few ideas of my own.'

'I'm sure you can.' It all sounded so polite and formal, when what she really wanted was to put her arms around him and have him hold her, kiss her, tell her that he had forgiven her, but that would be like trying to turn the clock back, and there was no way they could do that. The best she could hope for now was that they could form some sort of working relationship, even though every minute they spent together would be for her sweet agony. 'Luke, I want to. . .'

She broke off as Fred came into the room. He looked momentarily startled, then smiled at them both.

'Ah, I see you decided to tell Fran yourself what the new plan is. Good.'

'Plan? What plan?' She stared from one to the other, feeling apprehension shiver its cold way along her spine.

'I haven't got around to it yet, Fred. Why don't you fill her in on what's happening? I have a couple of things that need to be seen to before the programme goes out.'

He stood up and left the room with only the barest nod at both of them. Fran stared after him, then turned to Fred, her eyes bright with suspicion.

'All right, what's going on? Tell me.'

'Nothing drastic, love. There's just been a change in today's programme. We were going to run that tape you made after the planning-committee meeting, but in the light of recent events it seems unwise. So Hugh Jones has suggested that you do the follow-up to the programme with Calder.'

'Follow-up? You mean interview him again?'

Fred didn't appear to hear the horror in her voice, or if he did he managed to ignore it. 'Mmm. Good idea, isn't it, especially as his appointment as chairman has just been announced? Here, Debbie's put together a sample of points raised in some of those letters we've received. They should give you something to work from, although it's up to you what sort of things you want to ask, of course. Damned good luck that Calder happened to be available this morning, wasn't it?'

Good luck? No, it wasn't that. Fran knew that just as clearly as she knew her own name. Luck didn't enter into it. That scheming, conniving Capricorn had something planned!

* * *

'So, Mr Calder, you weren't really surprised at being asked to take over the job of chairman? You had an idea that it might happen?' Fran smoothed her notes out on the table, willing her hands to stay still when every bit of her was shaking. They had been on the air just five minutes now, five minutes that felt like five years! On the surface everything was going quite smoothly, with her asking the questions and Luke answering politely, but underneath the polite façade she could sense other emotions bubbling furiously.

'Perhaps surprised isn't the right word. I'd been given a hint that something like this could be on the cards when I was first approached.'

Luke smiled calmly back at her, crossing his long legs under the table so that his knee brushed against hers. Fran jumped as though she had been burnt, the papers rustling on the desk. She glared at him, then forced the annoyance from her voice. 'Is that one of the reasons why you were keen to invest in the first place, even one of the reasons why you decided to back the new housing development?'

'I have to admit that I prefer to be in charge of any given situation. I find it difficult to take orders, to be a follower rather than a leader, but I wouldn't have accepted if I wasn't confident that I could make some contribution to the station. However, my decision to back the new development came first. This was just a tempting addition to that.'

'I see. And how are your plans progressing? When will the building commence?'

'I can't put an exact date on it yet. We've hit a snag over one particular tract of land vital to the project.'

'What sort of a snag? Is someone reluctant to sell the

land to you so you can go ahead?' Her confidence was coming back now, so that she felt able to meet his gaze across the width of the small table.

Just for a moment he met her eyes, his own very dark and filled with something that made her heart start to beat rapidly, high in her throat, yet nothing could have prepared her for the shock of what he said.

'It isn't a question of that. Everyone we've approached has become convinced that the proposed development can only enhance the town. However, the land in question is now subject to a court order. It appears that it had been sold illegally by members of the council to a local businessman with the intention of defrauding the local ratepayers. Until the case comes to court and the real owner of the land is decided upon we can't go ahead. Fortunately, I had my suspicions about it right from the start, so I've been working closely with the police to help clear it up.'

Her head was spinning, filled with so many thoughts that it was impossible to sort one from another. He had been working with the police all along! Working on the side of truth and justice.

'I. . .' She swallowed down the joy she felt, her face glowing as she smiled at him. 'Then I'm sure the local community owes you a debt of gratitude, Mr Calder.'

'I don't want gratitude. I intend to make my home here in this town, and if I can do anything to ensure that the people here are treated fairly I shall do it. A principle I know you endorse.'

'I do indeed.' It was hard to stop the elation from showing, but Fran tried her best, knowing there would be time enough once they were off the air. 'So you'll be staying in the area, then?'

'Oh, yes. I intend to make my home here when I'm married.'

'Married!' It came out as an exclamation, and she heard the controller mutter something uncomplimentary through the headphones, but she didn't care. Her whole world felt as though it had just been rocked on its axis by the announcement, so that for long silent seconds she could only stare at him with pain in her eyes. So this was it, the end to all her dreams. Luke was getting married, and soon there would be a woman in his life who could lay claim to his love and who would have the right to love him back.

'Come on, Fran. Snap out of it!'

Fred's voice came through the headphones to her and she glanced towards the control-room, barely seeing the figures clustered behind the glass for the tears clouding her eyes. She felt as though she was dying, as though her heart was being ripped piece by piece into shreds, but she had to go on and finish the programme.

'Is. . .is this a sudden decision, Mr Calder?' she asked, looking down at her hands, which were folding the paper into a crumpled little heap.

'Mmm, very sudden. I only arrived at it this morning.'

That brought her head up, and she stared at him. 'This morning? But we. . .'

He continued as if she hadn't spoken, his voice dropping to a level of intimacy that suddenly made it feel as though they were alone, not being listened to by thousands of people. 'Very early this morning, to be precise. Some time around five-thirty.'

'Five-thirty?' She was starting to sound like a parrot,

repeating everything he said, but she couldn't seem to help herself.

'Yes. There's nothing quite like spending a night sleeplessly, going over one's problems. It seems to concentrate the mind, I find.' Luke reached across the desk and caught her nervous fingers between his own, smoothing them gently until they lay quietly against the ruined paper. 'There's only one snag, though.'

'What is it?' It took every bit of control she possessed to sit there and ask the question while her heart was beating like a drum.

'I haven't asked the lady in question yet.'

'You haven't?' The touch of his fingers on hers was playing havoc with her ability to think straight, and she knew he could see that from the faint gleam in his eyes, the way his hand tightened around hers.

'No. I think it would be a good idea if I did, don't you? So. . .will you marry me, Fran?'

'I. . .' All thoughts of where they were and what was happening fled abruptly as she stared at him with a shock that soon turned to joy as she saw the expression on his face.

'Twenty seconds, Fran. Nineteen. . .eighteen. . . seventeen. . .'

The controller started the countdown, yet still she sat there, unable to force the word from her lips. Luke covered the microphone with his hand and leant towards her, his lips just brushing hers in the tenderest of kisses before he whispered softly, 'I love you, Fran. So say yes and put us all out of our agony!'

'Yes!' She sensed rather than heard the collective sigh of relief that went up as her acceptance rang round the studio just a moment before the signature tune flowed through the headphones, signalling the end of the programme. Very slowly she took the headphones off and laid them carefully on the table, her eyes never leaving Luke's for a moment. He smiled slowly at her, standing up to come round the table and pull her gently to her feet and into his arms. Fran lifted her face for his kiss, holding him tightly, never wanting him to let her go again.

'Well, well. What a show!'

Colour flared into her face when Fred and the rest of the team stormed into the room, but when she tried to pull away from him Luke drew her back.

'I hope I didn't ruin your programme by that impromptu proposal, Fred?' There was little apology in Luke's voice or in the look he gave the other man, and Fred laughed.

'A fat lot you care! But no, you didn't. In fact, I'd raise bets that was one of the best shows we've ever put out! If you've any more good ideas like that then feel free to suggest them!'

'I'll bear it in mind. Now, if you don't mind, I'm going to whisk Fran away. After that very public proposal a few minutes' privacy are definitely called for.'

It took them almost twenty minutes to get out of the building as they fielded congratulations along the way. Finally they were outside, and Luke took her hand, kissing her quickly before urging her across the road to the car park and into his car. He made no move to start the engine but turned to face her, a fleeting, uncharacteristic uncertainty on his face.

'You're quite sure you want to marry me, Fran? I

sort of sprang it on you back in the studio, so you hardly had time to think.'

She smiled gently at him, letting him see all the love she had kept hidden from him before. 'I'm sure, Luke. I love you, and I can't imagine a life where you aren't the centre of it.'

'You'll never know how I've longed to hear you say that!' He pulled her to him, kissing her with a fierce, demanding passion that left her clinging to him. Slowly he eased away from her, stroking her cheek with his hand. 'I love you so much, Fran. I never imagined that I could feel this way about anyone, but I do.'

'When did you realise that you loved me?'

He smiled tenderly at the age-old question, his hand lingering against her face. 'The night you stayed at the house and we made love. It was like nothing I'd ever experienced before—so much feeling, so much exquisite joy. That's why I was so bitter the following day and spoke to you so cruelly. I felt pole-axed when you accused me of using you.'

'That's how I felt.' She met his eyes, not trying to hide the pain she had suffered. 'It almost broke me to hear you accuse me of going to bed with you to get a story. I loved you, Luke, and that's why I slept with you. I have to be honest and admit that I accepted the invitation to dinner to try to find out once and for all if you were involved with Martin, but that was because I needed to know, *needed* to prove your innocence, because I was falling in love with you. Hearing you on the telephone just seemed to confirm my worst fears, and I didn't stop to reason things through. I was hurting, so I hit out at you.'

'I can understand that now, but at the time. . .' Luke

looked away, but not before she had glimpsed the pain on his face. She took his hand, curling her fingers into his to lift it to her lips and kiss it.

'I'm sorry, Luke.'

'So am I, for hurting you. What you overheard that day did have something to do with Martin in a way. I'd hired a team of private investigators to keep an eye on you after your house was ransacked, and I was just ringing through to them to let them know where you were.'

'Private investigators? You were having me watched?' There was indignation in her voice, but he just smiled and bent to kiss her lips, unperturbed.

'Yes, and I make no apologies for it. You were getting yourself into a whole load of trouble, Fran, and I needed to ensure that there would be someone around to look after you when I couldn't be. I had no idea that it was Martin until you told me that morning. In a way it didn't surprise me, because I'd already had a taste of what he was up to with that land. Once you'd confirmed my suspicions it didn't take long to get to the bottom of the story. I made sure of that!'

There was a harsh note in his voice that made her shiver. 'It's hard to believe that anyone would go to such lengths, isn't it?'

'There are a lot of people around like him, unfortunately. But let's forget about him for now. There are other things I have in mind right now.'

Fran smiled seductively, snuggling against him. 'Such as?'

He kissed the tip of her nose. 'Such as going back to the house and making love to you until you start begging for mercy.'

'Sounds as if you've been making a few plans, Mr Calder!'

'Of course. Would you expect a cold, ruthless Capricorn like me to do anything else?'

'Cold? No, I wouldn't class you as that exactly, not in the right circumstances.' She slid her hands around his neck and drew his head down so that she could kiss him, feeling the way his heart began to thunder in his chest.

'Are you disputing all those facts poor Debbie dug up?'

'No. I think they're uncannily accurate. But there are other more complimentary ones attributed to your sign.'

'Been doing some research, have you?'

'Just a bit. Patience, determination, a good sense of humour. . .want me to go on?' Fran ticked them off on her fingers, loving him with her eyes.

Luke smiled. 'Not just now. Save it for later, when we have more time to spare.' He moved away from her and started the car, his dark eyes gleaming in a way that sent a delicious shudder tiptoeing along her spine. 'Right now this Capricorn can't wait to get one particular little Virgo into his bed—and do some research of his own!'

STARGAZING

YOUR STAR SIGN: CAPRICORN (December 23–January 20)

CAPRICORN is the tenth sign of the Zodiac, ruled by the planet Saturn and controlled by the element of Earth. These make you patient, prudent, reliable and—sometimes—selfish. Your need to be secure and in control and your high sense of achievement make you a natural climber of life, whose ultimate satisfaction is to fulfil a long-term goal—even if it is an uphill struggle!

Socially, Capricorns are reserved and selective in their choice of friends—but you do have a dry sense of humour and realise that fun and laughter can break down the barriers. At home, you like everything to be organised and carefully planned, though your strong sense of duty can be somewhat overbearing for those who live with you!

Your characteristics in love: Naturally shy and cautious at first, Capricorns are steady and careful in love and only when they feel more comfortable with partners do they reveal more of themselves. Nevertheless, you can make an excellent partner and your need for emotional security and permanency makes you very faithful and loyal in a relationship. For the Capricorn woman, relationships with the opposite sex can be tenuous because of your constant fear of rejection and getting hurt; being so vulnerable and fragile in love, you will give as good as you get. Therefore, you are likely to choose partners who will support you emotionally and boost your confidence sky-high!

Star signs which are compatible with you: Taurus, **Virgo**, **Scorpio**, and **Pisces** are the most harmonious, while **Cancer**, **Aries** and **Libra** provide you with a challenge. Partners born under other signs can be compatible, depending on which planets reside in their House of Personality and Romance.

What is your star-career? Work, for many Capricorns, is the greatest priority in life and, fired on with ambition and perseverance, they tend to have a definite and realistic goal at all times. Being kings of self-discipline and patience, positions which involve a high-level of responsibility and challenge will appeal to you, such as engineering, architecture, civil service, politics and surveying.

Your colours and birthstones: Capricorns tend to like subdued colours such as browns, greys and blacks to match their pessimistic nature.

Your birthstones are black jet and garnet; the latter gem comes in a variety of colours such as black, red, pink, orange or green and is known for its healing powers, especially for arthritis and, more recently, to aid couples without children emotionally and physically.

CAPRICORN ASTRO-FACTFILE

Day of the week: Saturday
Countries: India, Mexico, Afghanistan and Bulgaria
Flowers: Carnation, camellia & black poppy
Food: Coconut and beetroot; Capricorns love simple but good quality food and have an up-to-date knowledge of the most fashionable restaurants in town and the 'right' products to store in their kitchen cupboards.
Health: Disciplined in a regime of fitness and health, Capricorns tend to be the most long-lasting signs under the Zodiac—but be careful with your tendency to worry as you don't want to make excessive demands on yourself!

You share your star sign with these famous names:

Faye Dunaway	Diane Keaton
Annie Lennox	David Bowie
Rowan Atkinson	Paul Young
Dolly Parton	Rod Stewart
Maggie Smith	Muhammad Ali

Next Month's Romances

Each month you can choose from a wide variety of romance with Mills & Boon. Below are the new titles to look out for next month, why not ask either Mills & Boon Reader Service or your Newsagent to reserve you a copy of the titles you want to buy — just tick the titles you would like and either post to Reader Service or take it to any Newsagent and ask them to order your books.

Please save me the following titles:	Please tick	√
A DANGEROUS LOVER	Lindsay Armstrong	
RELUCTANT CAPTIVE	Helen Bianchin	
SAVAGE OBSESSION	Diana Hamilton	
TUG OF LOVE	Penny Jordan	
YESTERDAY'S AFFAIR	Sally Wentworth	
RECKLESS DECEPTION	Angela Wells	
ISLAND OF LOVE	Rosemary Hammond	
NAIVE AWAKENING	Cathy Williams	
CRUEL CONSPIRACY	Helen Brooks	
FESTIVAL SUMMER	Charlotte Lamb	
AFTER THE HONEYMOON	Alexandra Scott	
THE THREAD OF LOVE	Anne Beaumont	
SECRETS OF THE NIGHT	Joanna Mansell	
RELUCTANT SURRENDER	Jenny Cartwright	
SUMMER'S VINTAGE	Gloria Bevan	
RITES OF LOVE	Rebecca Winters	

If you would like to order these books in addition to your regular subscription from Mills & Boon Reader Service please send £1.70 per title to: Mills & Boon Reader Service, P.O. Box 236, Croydon, Surrey, CR9 3RU, quote your Subscriber No:..
(If applicable) and complete the name and address details below. Alternatively, these books are available from many local Newsagents including W.H.Smith, J.Menzies, Martins and other paperback stockists from 8th January 1993.

Name:..
Address:..
....Post Code:........................

To Retailer: If you would like to stock M&B books please contact your regular book/magazine wholesaler for details.

You may be mailed with offers from other reputable companies as a result of this application.
If you would rather not take advantage of these opportunities please tick box ☐

Love is in the Air...

Mills & Boon have commissioned four of your favourite authors to write four tender romances.

Guaranteed love and excitement for St. Valentine's Day

A BRILLIANT DISGUISE	-	Rosalie Ash
FLOATING ON AIR	-	Angela Devine
THE PROPOSAL	-	Betty Neels
VIOLETS ARE BLUE	-	Jennifer Taylor

Available from January 1993   PRICE £3.99

Mills & Boon

Available from Boots, Martins, John Menzies, W.H. Smith, most supermarkets and other paperback stockists.
Also available from Mills & Boon Reader Service, PO Box 236, Thornton Road, Croydon, Surrey CR9 3RU.

Mills & Boon

Four brand new romances from favourite Mills & Boon authors have been specially selected to make your Christmas special.

THE FINAL SURRENDER
Elizabeth Oldfield

SOMETHING IN RETURN
Karen van der Zee

HABIT OF COMMAND
Sophie Weston

CHARADE OF THE HEART
Cathy Williams

Published in November 1992   Price: £6.80

*Available from Boots, Martins, John Menzies, W.H. Smith, most supermarkets and other paperback stockists.
Also available from Mills & Boon Reader Service, PO Box 236, Thornton Road, Croydon, Surrey CR9 3RU.*

4 FREE Romances and 2 FREE gifts just for you!

You can enjoy all the heartwarming emotion of true love for FREE! Discover the heartbreak and the happiness, the emotion and the tenderness of the modern relationships in Mills & Boon Romances.

We'll send you 4 captivating Romances as a special offer from Mills & Boon Reader Service, along with the chance to have 6 Romances delivered to your door each month.

Claim your FREE books and gifts overleaf...

An irresistible offer from Mills & Boon

Here's a personal invitation from Mills & Boon Reader Service, to become a regular reader of Romances. To welcome you, we'd like you to have 4 books, a CUDDLY TEDDY and a special MYSTERY GIFT absolutely FREE.

Then you could look forward each month to receiving 6 brand new Romances, delivered to your door, postage and packing free! Plus our free Newsletter featuring author news, competitions, special offers and much more.

This invitation comes with no strings attached. You may cancel or suspend your subscription at any time, and still keep your free books and gifts.

It's so easy. Send no money now. Simply fill in the coupon below and post it to -
Reader Service, FREEPOST, PO Box 236, Croydon, Surrey CR9 9EL.

NO STAMP REQUIRED

Free Books Coupon

Yes! Please rush me 4 free Romances and 2 free gifts! Please also reserve me a Reader Service subscription. If I decide to subscribe I can look forward to receiving 6 brand new Romances each month for just £10.20, postage and packing free. If I choose not to subscribe I shall write to you within 10 days - I can keep the books and gifts whatever I decide. I may cancel or suspend my subscription at any time. I am over 18 years of age.

Ms/Mrs/Miss/Mr_____ EP31R

Address _____

_____

Postcode_____ Signature _____

Offer expires 31st May 1993. The right is reserved to refuse an application and change the terms of this offer. Readers overseas and in Eire please send for details. Southern Africa write to Book Services International Ltd, P.O. Box 42654, Craighall, Transvaal 2024. You may be mailed with offers from other reputable companies as a result of this application.

If you would prefer not to share in this opportunity, please tick box ☐